LiT
COMMENCEMENT

Maxwell F. Hurley

LiT
COMMENCEMENT

DOUBLE DRAGON

There is a shuffling of fear and anxiety when given the token to the future. Today's choices are no longer blissfully protected from tomorrow's consequences. The past years of experiences were just a tease of what lies ahead in the world. The realization of true human nature capability can be frightening.

CHAPTER ONE

Hiding her bruises and bloody clothes is never easy. Alex's mom, Michelle, was starting to get suspicious, especially when Alex began doing her own laundry. Her mom was asking why she was going through so many clothes. It was a blessing for Alex that the Council gave her a clothing allowance for her gear...as long as she didn't go crazy. Although when Father Joe gave her that council card before he left for Moscow, he kept insisting she find some tougher clothing for fighting Infiltrators. It made sense, but Alex still had to be herself for the last three weeks of school.

For one of the last times, Alex pulled into the school parking lot. A feeling of sadness and anxiety hit her, knowing in just a little while, she was no longer going to be here. Komptin was sleeping in the backseat of her car. The Council rushed the paperwork to make Komptin her PTSD dog. Which it was slightly true; she had adopted him the night Osiah died. He didn't just die; Vandor, the Conduit of the Dark, murdered him. The image of him thrusting his hand through Osiah's back, coming out of his chest, was something Alex could never forget. Osiah, a former Dark Sentry Warrior, died trying to save them, to save his love, the Conduit of Lite, Celestial. Upon his sacrifice was a battle like Alex had never seen before. Despite the Guardians of the Conduit of Lite helping, Alex didn't think she did too badly. That night, she had killed her first Demon.

Unfortunately, that particular Demon was her best friend's dad. That bastard killed Sara that very night, but Alex was able to get her revenge. She disposed of that son of bitch. But not without a consequence of the battle. She pulled down the visor to look at the scar on her neck before putting on her leather collar. She had convinced her dad and the police an unknown assailant had attacked her.

There were reports of an up-and-coming cult that Sara's dad was trying to join. Part of their initiation was to attack random people. It explained why Sara was killed, Alex's bruises, and, of course, the attack on Mole. Speaking of whom, he had just pulled into the parking lot with Anne driving. Alex watched Mole try to get out of the passenger side of Anne's car. She rushed over to the car as quickly as she could. "Don't, don't do it."

"I'm fine," Mole tried to get up, using the door as leverage.

Anne got out of the car to get the wheelchair from the trunk of her car. "He's a tough guy, Alex." Her chipmunk smile towards her boyfriend was a clear indicator of her feelings towards Alex's brother. Anne carefully rolled the chair behind Mole. Alex, of course, didn't miss the detail that Anne never calls him by his nickname anymore. It was always his real name, Kale. They were so cute together. The three of them entered the school, where people were still giving Alex and Mole sympathetic looks and whispering tall tales to each other of what happened. The two of them really didn't care, but it bothered Anne a bit.

With Sara's murder and her father 'missing,' there was high school gossip always flying, but Alex and Anne knew the truth. On top of that, Roger just seemed to disappear from school after attacking her newly found sibling, almost killing him. Alex just thanked God that Mole would be able to walk again. Every hunt she goes on, she prays she finds Roger to take revenge for her brother. That Demon changed his life forever. But in a weird way, it bonded the three of them. The trio were sitting in the corner of the hallway. Alex had her Apollo in her hand while the caring couple next to her were taking turns sipping a hot tea. Mole's face every time he took a mouthful made Alex laugh. "Not good?"

"It's disgusting." He forced it down.

"Why are you drinking it?" Alex grabbed it from his hands to smell it. It was revolting. She quickly shook it off from her head before handing it back to him. "All yours."

Anne took possession of it after Mole took a sip. "It's a great source of tannins, with a touch of cinnamon and clover that has volatile oils that are antimicrobial and soothing for his stomach with all the pills he's taking." Anne took another sip before giving it back to Mole. "Now drink up." She gave a small chuckle as he forced it down.

Alex had time before first period. "It's weird knowing we'll be out of here in a bit."

"Personally, I'm happy we only have a few weeks left, and then college." Mole handed the drink back to Anne. "I can't do this anymore."

Anne grabbed it without saying anything. Just a facial expression of compassion with her high cheekbone smile. "I don't know, I'm going to miss it."

Kale busted out laughing, "We almost died here."

"Year isn't over." Alex smacked Mole on the back of the head. Then she playfully made the impression that it was Anne. She went down to scratch Komptin behind the ears. The massive German Shepherd liked to be in the school with all the people. It was rare he got to be in places with people that didn't consist of being on guard for the Dark. He just stayed in the back of Alex's classrooms, instantly falling asleep. There was just one time he alerted.

Alex was taking a sociology test when they caught a sense of the Dark nearby. It didn't feel like an Infiltrator. It might have been a Demon. It definitely wasn't Vandor. His sense of Dark was so strong it overpowered anything around him. Demons almost had the same sense as an Infiltrator, but a lot less dense. Alex's ability to sense Demons wasn't actually toned in enough. She still had to wait for them to use their powers before sensing them. She had to really concentrate on people, staring directly at them to be able to try to sense any Dark. This particular sense of the Dark felt different. She can't remember where she felt it before, but it seemed familiar. It didn't last long before whatever it was dissipated.

They were just about to break for first period when Mr. Dupel approached the group. The

10

Guidance Counselor for the school had been pressuring Alex to come see him. "I'm trapped." Alex halfway joked as she tried to get out of this situation.

Mole put his backpack on his lap. "Anne, I think now would be a good time to roll on over to class."

Anne pushed her wavy brown hair back. She gave him a quick kiss on the cheek before going behind him to push his chair to class. "Perfect, I can tell you about these new herbal supplement hard candies I found online," Anne teased as they both went down the hall.

"That's just mean," Alex yelled as she was about to leave when Mr. Dupel caught up to her.

"Alex," The counselor blocked her escape. He was the youngest teacher in the school, a nice man who really cared about the students. Almost like it was his personal mission to make things better in their lives. When Sara died, he set up counseling sessions with the students, was key in setting up the school service, and personally made it a point to talk to Sara's boyfriend, Robbie, to see how he was holding up. He also organized the school program to help any kid with a tragic event, mainly trying to get their lives together. He was instrumental in helping to push through the papers to keep Komptin in the classrooms with Alex. It was nice to have a teacher who seemed to go the extra mile for the student's well-being.

"Mr. Dupel," Her black braided hair tugged a bit as she leaned against the wall. "What up?"

"We still have to make an appointment to go over your plans after graduation." He greeted some other students as the two of them came by "Hey, Jack, we need to meet up for that paperwork for State."

"I won't forget, Mr. D," Jack pointed his fingers like a gun at him.

Alex just shook her head, thinking about how she had been making out with him just last weekend. Mr. Dupel's fingers snapping in front of her face caught her attention. "Oh, sorry, that future thing, right."

"You are a strange one, Alex. Once in a while you've got a great focus on you, almost death-defying, but your carefree attitude just pushes your potential out." he pulled out his phone. "So, checking my schedule, I can get you out of fourth period to go over your plans."

"Taken care of," Alex checked her watch. "Not too worried about it. St. Michaels gave me a scholarship."

"Yes, interesting on how such a prestigious Catholic church would give someone with a 2.3 GPA a full ride who's not even Catholic." Mr. Dupel's attention got distracted as two kids were standing on the windowsill of the hallway. "Hey, get down." The kids succumbed to his wish.

Alex took a peek down the hall along with Komptin. "Work scholarship, I guess."

"I suppose, anyways, I have to sign off some paperwork for a Father Carl Gray and Thomas Altomer." He handed her a piece of paper from inside his suit jacket pocket. "Here, this will get you out of fourth period."

"Really? Couldn't you get me out of sixth period instead?" Alex grabbed the note.

"Have a good day, Alex," he good-humoredly shooed her away with a hand gesture. Alex was about to leave when a classmate of hers approached with Shawn. Alex recognized him as a junior, but he made the varsity football team as the starting.... something. Alex didn't really know, or care. All she knew was his name was Hayden. "Hey, what's up?"

Shawn was about to say something, but in a rare form of empathy, he just said, "Alex, I'm really sorry about Sara. She was one of the good ones."

Alex accepted his gesture. "Thanks, Shawn." Then, Alex felt uncomfortable all of a sudden. She looked around as that weird sense of Dark was there. Her nerves shot up, but then it suddenly vanished.

"Well, I have to get to class, later." Shawn knuckle-bumped Hayden.

"Later, Shawn," Leaving just Alex and Hayden in the corner of the hallway.

Alex grabbed her book bag from the ground. "I need to get going, don't really want to be late with only a couple of weeks left."

"What class do you have?" Hayden was trying to spark conversation.

"Mythology," Alex rolled her eyes.

"Oh, my class is right next door. Can I walk with you?" Hayden motioned.

"Free world," Alex grabbed Komptin's leash. "Come on boy…. you too, Komptin," she teased him.

"Funny." Hayden started following Alex. "So, lucky you, graduating this year."

"Yep." Alex started towards class. "Next year will go by fast."

"Maybe. I'm hoping Brooke will be getting into the same college or nearby." Hayden was making small chit-chat, but it was obvious he had another agenda on his mind.

"Oh, you're dating Brooke Williams?" Alex was a little disappointed. This boy was actually a little cute.

"About a month now." Hayden shied a bit when he smiled. "She keeps me in line."

"That's sweet. What're your plans for college?" Alex was coming close to her classroom.

"I want to go into criminal justice. I wouldn't mind being an FBI agent; that sounds pretty cool." Hayden let her know.

"You go on with your bad self," Alex sarcastically encouraged him. "I wouldn't want anything to do with any government types. Always so uptight."

"To each their own," Hayden stopped in front of his classroom. "Anyway, I wanted to get with you regarding your job. I think it would look good on a college application that I was working at a church. Is there any way you can put in a good word for me to take over your position when you go to college?"

Alex had to prevent herself from laughing. "I don't think you'd want it."

"Well, it's only for a year. Can you put in a good word?" Hayden was on the verge of begging.

"I'll see what I can do." Alex escaped into her morning class with no intention of fulfilling his request.

CHAPTER TWO

Alex moved her head to the music she was listening to as her headphones were on full volume. It'd been a long day, so she was happy to leave school with Komptin loyally by her side. The school had a feeling of relief as it was a gorgeous day, and a Friday to boot. She had just stepped out of the building on her way to the parking lot when she got a feeling something wasn't right. It wasn't the Dark, but something was off. Then, a forceful tap on her shoulder that was in no way friendly.

Alex closed her eyes, knowing this wouldn't be a pleasant conversation, no matter who was behind her. In a flash, she ran through all the people she had pissed off lately; she couldn't think of anybody who wasn't supernatural. Maybe, with a bit of luck, it was Roger. That brought a smile to her face; it was time to settle a score.

The Lite Sentry turned around to see a blonde girl wearing a pair of jean shorts and a t-shirt that read, "Heart's Desire" with the shape of one around the words. She had a look of determination in her blue eyes as she stared down the small girl in black weaved hair, wearing dark makeup.

"Brooke, what's going on?" Alex sensed some kids were already starting to gather around, getting ready to watch a potential fight. Brooke was a popular girl: attractive, smart, and as far as Alex knew, a genuinely nice person. But that doesn't seem like the case now.

"Stay away from him. I don't want your disgusting claws into my boyfriend." She confidently took a step forward towards Alex.

Normally, Alex would have already started swinging, but not in this fight. She didn't know how much damage she could do to someone who wasn't Dark. As far as Alex could tell, she wasn't under their evil influence. Or maybe she was? Alex squinted her eyes as she studied the angry blonde in front of her.

"What are you doing, you freak?" Brooke had a disgusted look on her face as she wanted Alex to throw a punch.

The Lite Sentry couldn't sense anything from Brooke. She was just angry at Alex for something. "Look, Brooke. I have no idea what you're talking about."

Brooke stepped forward to close the gap with Alex. "I saw you talking to him this morning. Stay away from him. I know how you go through guys, you slut."

"Excuse me?" Now Alex had enough as she dropped her bag on the ground. Komptin barked in warning, but it didn't help Alex back down. "Brooke, watch yourself. There is nothing positive coming out of this for you."

"You think I'm scared of a little goth whore, who does it with every guy who talks to her?" Brooke stepped back in a stance that meant she was about to strike.

The crowd was now much bigger, that included Mole and Anne. Mole saw that Mr. Pogolowski and Dupel were rushing to get through the crowd.

"Ms. Johnson, Ms. Williams." Mr. Pogolowski came in between them. "You guys better be discussing the finals coming up."

"Far from it. This little hormonal hussy is about to get a very hard lesson." Alex was now in full-out anger.

"Alex!" Anne yelled out to her.

Alex turned to Anne, who was standing behind Kale's wheelchair. Anne pointed to the front of her throat, reminding Alex of a priest's collar. The Lite Sentry reluctantly backed down.

Mr. Pogolowski pointed to Brooke. "Go on, Ms. Williams. Go home."

"Watch it, Alex. I mean it." Brooke pushed her finger on Alex's chest. Alex immediately pushed it off, about to attack, but Mr. Pogolowski stepped in between them. Brooke just stared at the two faculty members.

Mr. Dupel rubbed his head. "Come on, Alex. Let's go." He pointed to the inside of the school.

"I didn't do anything. This is some bullshit!" Alex started to argue as she grabbed her backpack from the ground. Mr. Pogolowski snapped his fingers and pointed to the inside of the building. "Ugh!" Alex grabbed Komptin's leash. "Come on, boy." Alex followed the overweight teacher back into the school with Mr. Dupel behind her. The three of them stopped at the first empty classroom, leaving the door open.

"Are you okay?" Mr. Dupel asked as he sat down at the teacher's desk.

"I'm fine," Alex gritted her teeth.

Mr. Pogolowski made it over to the window to see the audience of kids dispersing from the potential fight. "You can leave in about five minutes."

Alex was a bit confused. "I'm not in trouble?"

"Just wanted to diffuse the situation," Mr. Dupel reached into his pocket and pulled out a piece of gum.

"No punches were thrown, minus your language; there's nothing really you did wrong." Mr. Pogolowski turned to his student. "You can go, Ms. Johnson."

"Thanks," Alex felt a burden suddenly relieved.

"Alex, if there is anything you want to talk about, my door is always open." Mr. Dupel watched the future graduate gather her belongings. He handed her a small card. "This is a hotline where I volunteer. It allows kids to just call to talk. Completely confidential. If you just want to get anything off your chest."

Alex grabbed the card. "Thanks."

***

The food Alex got from Marty's didn't even make it out of the parking lot. The fast-food joint made the best double cheeseburgers; Alex ate two of them, plus a large fry. Inside her backpack was the secret ingredient to her favorite treat. She opened up a can of an Apollo Energy Drink to mix in a large vanilla milkshake.

On her way to the church, she kept thinking about the fight she'd almost gotten into. Alex didn't understand why Brooke was so upset that she was talking with Hayden. All they talked about was her job at the church. Plus, it was obvious that he had it bad for the angry blonde. Not that it wasn't Alex's problem; she was already late for work. Father Hanley needed her to print off the church programs for Sunday, and it had to get done today.

When she pulled into the parking lot, she let Komptin out of the backseat, where he was in a playful mood. The German Shepherd started to tease Alex by jumping around her, barking, and nipping at her. The Lite Sentry didn't back down. "Oh, you wanna go?" She laughed. Alex forgot she was on church property as Komptin easily tackled her onto the ground. Alex was half laughing, the other half trying to show she wasn't hurt. "I forgot how strong you actually are." To make up for the humility check, she was greeted with licks from her massive friend. "Forgiven." She put her arms around his neck for an immense hug.

The replacement priest for Father Joe came out of the church prepared for a run. He seemed like a good man, but he had no idea of Alex's true job at the church. He just thought she was a teen trying to get her life on track. He approached her as he was fumbling with his music pods. Alex wasn't going to lie; he was a very attractive man for someone in his fifties. "Hello, Alex. You're late," he teased as he pointed to his watch.

"Some girl at school almost got a painful lesson." Alex got off the ground to brush herself off.

Father Hanley sighed, "What happened?"

"Not my fault. Really. You can ask the teachers that prevented the fight." Alex defended herself to the new priest. "Wouldn't have lasted long anyway." The Lite Sentry grabbed her backpack from her car.

"They never do." Father Hanley checked his running watch. "I'm going to go for a quick run before youth group. Can you double-check the program for any errors I emailed you before printing?"

"No problem," she winked at him. Then, a feeling of guilt came over her. Why would she wink at a priest? She hoped it didn't come off that she found him attractive.

"Okay." He was just about to start his music before he stopped himself. "By the way, do you know Father Tom Altomer?"

"Nope. Why?" Alex grabbed her milkshake from the cup holder.

"No reason." The priest ensured his music pods were secure.

"What do you listen to anyways?" Alex was curious on what was on a priest's music playlist.

Father Hanley smiled, "The best era of music, ultimate eighties pop. Just put the programs in a box for the altar boys."

She gave him a thumbs-up. "Enjoy your run." Alex turned to look at the building that was her sanctuary. She wasn't going to lie to herself. The warmth she felt from the Lite when inside the building was one heck of a motivator to take her time with her work.

**

Alex finished reviewing the formatting of the church programs. She always made it a personal goal to find something wrong with the program. She never could. Now, she was just enjoying the peace of sitting at Osiah's, or she guessed it was her desk now. Her feet were on the old wooden desk as she was twirling around her Apollo energy drink in her glass. The only sound was the ice as it hit the cold sides of the glass. Komptin was sleeping under the open window as Osiah's purple star shined above in the sky. Alex just told her parents she was going to a party after work, but she knew the truth.

She slammed down the rest of her drink and went to the closet to get ready for the night. The clothes she brought from home for hunting weren't the best, but it was all she had. Alex put on a pair of thin spandexes with a dark blue skirt over it and a black shirt with a bunch of skulls printed on it and touched up her makeup in the mirror's reflection. In the background, Komptin was stretching as he started to wake up.

The massive German Shepherd came up to her and nudged her lightheartedly. She, in turn, bumped him back. "Let's go protect that Balance." The two of them drove until she had a small sense of the Dark in a woodland area. It must have been close to one in the morning of her trudging through the woods. Still, no sign of any Infiltrators. *"That was disappointing."* Alex decided to head back to the car. The two hunters decided to swing by the park where Alex had her first Infiltrator kill.

A small light was illuminating in the distance, along with a whole bunch of laughter. There was a fire going in the pavilion's fireplace, so Alex wanted to check it out. A small get-together with some of the kids from school seemed to be in full swing. Alex joined the mixture of juniors and a couple of seniors. Shawn was talking to Cindy in the corner. Well, they were doing a little bit more than exchanging words. Some of Anne's friends were in a clutter of deep discussion. Alex casually came in behind them to grab a drink from the cooler. Just her luck, an Apollo Energy Drink was sitting there waiting for her.

"We really need to talk to Anne," Evelyn was trying to convince her friends.

Angela nodded in agreement. "She is far too smart with a bright future to get involved with someone like Mole."

That got Alex's attention as she now motioned for Komptin to stay.

"Do you think she's just with him as a fling before college?" Angela took a sip of her drink.

Another one of Anne's friends, Chloe, checked her phone. "And when he fell off his bike and got hurt, she probably got a Florence Nightingale effect going on. She's probably blinded."

"Excuse me! Mole didn't fall off his bike. He was attacked by a monster. Nearly killed him."

Alex's voice was a little more forceful than she wanted.

The girls jumped at the sight of an angered fighter behind them, ready to throw hands. They were flustered with a mixture of fear as they didn't know what Alex would do. Chloe was the first to speak, "Alex, look. I'm sorry, but we're just looking out for our friend."

"As am I." Alex didn't back down. She had to calm herself down as she felt her arms start to tingle.

"We should go. Anne is expecting us in the morning." Angela gathered her friends before Alex did anything. "Let us be the friends that Anne needs. Her future isn't with Kale Moler." The group went off to discuss their intervention.

Alex stepped forward to go have a physical 'talk' with them, but Komptin pulled on her shirt with his mouth. "I know, I know." Alex saw that Hayden and Brooke were in the corner of the pavilion talking. It probably would be wise to stay away from the two of them.

"Drink?" A voice came up behind Alex.

Alex smiled at the long-haired brunette man. She lifted up an Apollo energy drink. "Got one." He was cute, with a certain bad boy sense to him. The flannel shirt open with a black t-shirt with a band's name on it just completed his impression on Alex. The ripped jeans were just the icing on the cake. "I'm Alex."

"I'm Don." He took a sip of the beer he was holding.

"I've seen you around," Alex smiled at him.

"Oh, do I feel special that Alex Johnson noticed me?" He teased her, "How do I rate?"

Alex eyed him up and down. "So far, pretty good, with the potential of your stock rising." She lost track of time as the two of them were talking before Don suggested the two of them go to his car. Alex didn't object.

The squeeze of her hand was all she needed to start to follow him to his car. Komptin got up to follow Alex, but she turned around to tell him to stop with just a lift of her finger. The mammoth dog succumbed to her wishes but didn't take his eyes off her. Alex got into the backseat of the car along with Don. It didn't take long before Alex climbed onto his lap. She grabbed Don by the face as she continued to kiss him. There were no objections as his hands began to touch the bare skin on her back. It was with ease that he unsnapped her bra. Don encouraged Alex to start taking off his flannel shirt. The car windows were starting to steam up when Alex got blasted with a stale sense of air from an infiltration taking place. "Damn it."

"What? What is it?" Don continued to know his intentions towards Alex with her ear.

Alex shivered from the slight nibble on her ear lobe. "I have to go," Alex got off Don's lap as she snapped her bra back together.

"Are you kidding me?" Don slammed his head back on the seat. "Come on, just a little longer."

Alex wouldn't have minded continuing, but that sense of Dark was a little bit too close for comfort. "No, I really need to go." Alex put her shoes back on and got out of the car. With a loud whistle, she signaled for Komptin to join her. He came running up to her as she continued to calmly stroll down the dark road. There was a spot where she was able to duck into the brush. This provided cover to watch over the party to ensure no Infiltrator decided to have a field day.

Don came out of the car, no doubt upset. His friends met up with him, full out laughing. "Dude," one of them was clearly intoxicated. "It's pretty bad if you strike out with Alex Johnson."

Don laughed at himself. "No shit. Get me a beer." He went off with his friends to enjoy the fire.

A weird feeling came over Alex. A quick sense of guilt came over her, or was it shame? For some reason, Komptin inched his way closer to her, as if comforting her. Alex reached up with her hand to start scratching behind his ears. She didn't have time to worry about it as she was just here to protect her classmates. One by one, the cars started to disappear. She noticed Shawn and Cindy left together, as well as Brooke and Hayden. There was something off about Brooke and Hayden's relationship. Alex couldn't pinpoint it, but there was something wrong.

The last of her classmates put out the fire in the pavilion before grabbing the cooler to take off for the night. Alex got up from her overwatch post and motioned for Komptin to join her. She circled around the park, keeping to the woods. There was a log in her route she climbed over and some branches that she dodged. It was still a little cool when the sun left the valley, which was nice.

She caught a faint sense of familiarity in the presence of evil that just hit her. This was no doubt an Infiltrator. Alex continued her hunt, where she got into the swampy part of the woods, a precursor to the lake. The fog from the swamp was starting to fill the empty spaces between the trees. The stronger sense of the Infiltrator she was hunting hit her so hard that for a split second, she got a bit lightheaded. Alex grabbed onto a tree to maintain her balance. She lifted her head to see a pair of red eyes staring at her with a low growl emanating.

"Komptin, circle around. Make sure we're not interrupted." Alex had her eyes in a continuous glow as she faced her foe from across the moist bog. Komptin morphed into his hunting form as his eyes, too, were glowing with the power of the Lite. With a massive roar, he took off into the woods to make sure Alex's fight wasn't interrupted.

Alex trudged towards the red glowing eyes of hate. The black soldier of the Dark mirrored her movements. Alex's glowing, neon-blue hands reflected in the small pools of murky water. The Infiltrator went from trudging on all fours to standing on two feet. It was bigger than the last one she fought; its claws ready to tear into Alex's body. The Lite Sentry cracked her neck as it started running towards her.

Alex side-stepped and created a Lite Beam, pushing the creature into a tree. Alex went to attack, but her foot got stuck in the swamp mud. The Infiltrator slowly turned his head to lock its hateful red eyes with Alex. "Oh shit." The beast swung its massive arm. She managed to put her arm up to guard against the massive blunt force, but it wasn't enough. The impact got her out of the vacuum of the mud, but at a cost. The weightlessness of her body flying through the air was a split-second oasis before the inevitable impact of the foul stench of the swamp.

It was going to take quite a while for all this mud to wash out her hair and clothes. She stood up and noticed her pants were ripped from colliding with the sticks on the natural floor. The beast ran at her again, but she managed an uppercut underneath its pointed jaw, slamming its open mouth shut. It was the beast's turn to go crashing onto the swamp's surface. There was no time for celebration; Alex went on the offensive. She grabbed a wooden log lying in the mud and swung against the body of the Infiltrator. The unnatural bending of its body was caused by smashing into a nearby tree.

Its body was limp as it eyed Alex. She took this moment to regain her composure. The sense of lacking strength in the creature gave Alex the permission she was seeking to dispose of it. As she prepared to dispose of the creature, she saw weakness in its eyes. She thought she saw fear as it started to cower. Alex felt guilty. It was just a slave to their master's wishes. A quick feeling of empathy for the hurt creature overcame Alex as she put her arms down. "It's okay, really. I'm not going to hurt you." Alex put her hand out in a friendly gesture. She gazed into the creature's frightened eyes. "Shh, it's okay."

Pure thoughts of hope rushed through her head as she thought of the possibilities of the ability to convert Infiltrators to the Lite. That was quickly interrupted as its eyes turned to a glowing red. It quickly swiped at Alex with its claws. Alex managed to dodge out of the way from the death blow, but her poor lack of experience came at a cost. Not only were her clothes ripped, but also the skin on her body was sliced open. "Son of bitch!" Alex's eyes glowed blue as she formed a Lite Spear. There wasn't much effort as she thrust the spear into the creature's body. It disappeared as it melted, combining with the muddy surface.

Alex checked her side as a mixture of blood and mud soaked through her frayed clothing. She cringed in pain as she turned around to see Komptin sitting on top of a log, lying down in his purple gargoyle hunting form. His legs were crossed as if he was watching the show—her ignorance of the evil of the Infiltrators. "I know, I know; lesson learned." She pressed her hand against the wound as she petted her hunting companion with the other.

CHAPTER THREE

Alex thrust her hand into the spine of the werewolf, and she picked it up before slamming it against the ground. She completed her victory with a vicious scream over the carcass. "And that's how I do that." Alex laughed as she put down her video game controller to take a sip of her Apollo. She and Mole played video games for the past hour this Saturday morning.

"You suck." Kale grabbed a sports bottle filled with water. "Speaking of which, was last night fun for you?"

"Why? What did you hear?" Alex put down her drink.

"Dan heard from Robbie, who heard it from Shawn, that you hooked up with some junior last night." Kale restarted the game. They continued their fight on the television screen.

"You guys gossip more than a bunch of old ladies at breakfast." This time, it was Mole who was gaining the advantage.

"You should try to get to know someone before giving them the goods." Mole frantically hit the button on his controller, knocking Alex's elf warrior onto the ground. The werewolf jumped on the elf and tore into the body. Pixelated blood splattered on the screen as wolf howls echoed. "And that is how *I* do it." He shoved the controller in Alex's face.

She playfully pushed it away. "Come on, you big ape." Alex slammed down her drink before the game reset. They continued to fight before Alex paused the game. "Can I ask you something?"

"What's up?"

Alex leaned back on the couch. "Have you and Anne...?" She made a sexual motion with her hands.

Her brother pushed down her hands. "First of all, tactful. Second, why are you asking that?"

"Just curious," Alex stared forward in deep thought.

Mole got serious. "No, frankly speaking. I don't want to."

"Why? You don't find her attractive? Was it that big male nurse at the hospital who was giving you a sponge bath?" Alex snapped herself out of her trance.

"He really did have soft hands." He fought back laughing. "No, it's not that. Anne...is, well. Anne is special, and I don't want to ruin what we have just because I have raging hormones." Mole reached over to take some of his pain pills. He saw that Alex had a concerned look on her face. "My mom only gives me enough for the day. She hides the rest."

Alex nodded with support. "Good." Alex switched back to talking to Anne. "Now, your relationship, how do you know not to go so far?"

"I don't know, just go with your feelings." Mole saw a concerned Alex. For a moment, she had a look of regret on her face. "Alex, maybe if you just take your time with a guy, let them know how special you are...you'll see it too."

Alex turned to Mole. "You're such a sappy Hallmark card."

Kale laughed, "And you're a venereal pharmaceutical commercial waiting to happen." He poked her side.

"OW!" Alex flinched in pain.

"What's with you?" Mole was eyeing Alex's side. "Is it that time of month?"

"I had a hysterectomy, you moron. I can't get my period." Alex teased him.

"How am I supposed to know what goes on down there?" Kale pointed to her lower torso with his game controller. "That's not a subject guys normally talk about to each other." He hit play on her video game controller and continued to beat Alex's character down again. "I don't like to brag, but I'm kind of awesome." He held out his hand. "Help me up."

Alex got off the couch to help Mole. She had to be careful with him. She could still feel how fragile he was. "You okay?"

"I'm fine. I have to take a leak. It takes me a bit to get over there." Mole started to limp over to the downstairs bathroom.

Alex went into the kitchen to grab another energy drink and ice. Komptin perked his ears toward the window. Alex could see Anne's car pulling up the driveway. Mole's girlfriend got out of the car, holding a box.

"Hey, Alex. I just picked up Kale's graduation gown from the school. Thought I'd drop it by." Anne came into the house–very comfortably–Alex mentally noted. "Where's Kale?"

"Ensuring the sewage system in this town is still working." Alex motioned with her head. They both looked to the bathroom as the toilet flushed. "Wash your hands."

"Shut up," Mole yelled from the bathroom. The door opened, and Mole instantly smiled when he saw Anne standing in the doorway. "Now I'm glad I actually washed my hands."

"Gross," Anne chuckled as she went up to him for a kiss.

"Seriously, Mole, what's with these Hallmark moments?" Alex teased as she secretly admired the two of them.

Anne smirked, "You'll have yours someday, sweetie."

"Nope. Not happening. I'm not going to be some chintzy TV Hallmark movie where they have the same plot: two opposites forced together, flirt with each other, cheesy gestures, and then fall in love at Christmas." Alex playfully put her finger down her throat to act as if she was going to vomit.

Anne laughed, "I'm sure it won't go like that." She turned to Kale. "I have to go home and finish up my essay." Anne was all excited. "I'm hoping I can get into this advanced history program." She crossed her fingers.

"You got this," Alex winked. "Hey, do you want to meet up later? I need some help picking out an outfit."

Anne nodded. "I can do that. I can pick you up if you want?"

"Meet me at the church at five." Alex whistled for Komptin as he came to her side. "I'm going to have lunch with my parents, and then I have to go to the church to finish up some stuff."

***

The lead altar boy picked up the programs from Alex. It didn't go well; apparently, he was friends with Donny. He just gave her that 'I know what you did' grin. Alex didn't say anything to him as she handed him the programs. She didn't feel like staying there while the older altar boys performed ceremony practice. So, she decided to hide in her office. The late spring nights were nice, but there were times she wished it was darker faster. She was in a somber mood and wanted to sit alone in the dark.

It was quiet upstairs in her office as she drank her Apollo with ice. Komptin was sleeping hard underneath the window. For some reason, it gave Alex a bit of solace. There was a slight knock on her door before Father Hanley peeked in on Alex. She slightly waved him in but didn't move any other part of her body. Komptin peeked with one eye at the priest before falling back asleep.

Father Hanley sat down on the brown leather chair beside her office door. "How's it going?"

"Ever get that feeling that you don't know what you are feeling?" She swirled her iced energy drink in her glass as she stared out the window.

"Alexithymia." Father Hanley adjusted himself in the chair.

She just moved her eyes towards the priest. "My full name is Alexandria."

Father Hanley tried not to laugh at the innocence of the young lady. "Wanna talk about it?"

"We just did." Alex adjusted her stance. "What's on your mind, padre?"

"I just got off the phone with St. Michaels, the college you will be attending. They need some information from your guidance counselor." He tossed the paper card over on Alex's desk.

"I'll take care of it." Alex put the card in her book bag next to her on the floor. Alex saw that Father Hanley wasn't himself. "Are you okay?"

"I'm fine. Confession can really take it out of you sometimes." He wiped his face with his hand. "That needs to get done before graduation." He pointed to her book bag.

"I won't forget." As Anne knocked, Alex saw that Komptin's head perked up at the door. "Hey."

"Am I interrupting?" Anne innocently asked.

"No, not at all. Father Hanley." He got up to shake Anne's hands.

"Anne McClure." She returned the handshake. "Are you ready, or do you need more time?"

"Am I good, Father?" Alex was already getting her stuff together.

"You're good. I need to make a couple of phone calls anyway. It was nice meeting you, Anne."

"Likewise, Father." Anne stepped into the office so Father Hanley could leave. "Ready to go, sweetie?"

Alex whistled for Komptin as he eagerly joined the two girls on their shopping expedition. They ended up in the mall on the other side of Westington. Alex was going through the clothes in the sporting goods section of the shopping center.

Anne was kind of confused on her store choice. "I never pictured you picking outfits from here."

"I need to find hunting clothes." Alex lifted up a camouflage shirt. "Just not a big fan of this style." The sound of metal hangers scraping against the shiny metal racks meant she wasn't having any luck.

"So, make your own." Anne lifted up a pair of black hiking boots. "These are cute, practical." Anne flipped over to see the price. "And very expensive."

"I do like them." Alex put them in the cart. Anne took a look in the cart along with the pair of black pants Alex threw in. "I have the Council credit card." Alex's attention was caught on a dark blue long-sleeved shirt. "This is nice."

"So, what made you come to the decision of getting new clothes?" Anne lifted up a bright biking outfit but put it away. She turned to Alex, who got her attention. Anne watched as Alex lifted up her shirt and saw the wound on Alex's side. "Oh my God, did you get that checked out?"

"Trust me, it was a lot worse last night." Alex picked up another dark shirt, but this one was green. She threw it in the cart along with a purple one.

"That happened last night." Anne quietly tried to keep her shock level low.

"One of the pleasures of having the Lite in you." Alex scanned the area. "I need something else. Something that makes me, me." Alex scanned the store but couldn't find anything. Anne was going through the clothes but not really paying attention. "What's on your mind?"

"Oh, Chloe and the others kind of cornered me this morning. They felt the need to warn me about Kale." Anne held up an Iron Man training outfit. She saw that Alex was getting upset. "Don't be mad at them. They weren't attacking Kale…it was more making sure I knew what I was doing."

Alex tightened her lips and tapped her fingers on the clothing rack. "Anne, what is your intention when you go to school?"

Anne had her eyes start to get glossy. "Honestly, I don't want to break up. For some reason, I just know I'm going to be with him for the rest of his life, and nothing would make me happier."

"So, it's just not a fling for the summer?" Alex finally flat-out asked her.

Anne smiled. "Alex, there are two people outside my family that I can't afford to lose. Luckily, they're both related to each other."

Alex got a lump in her throat. "Okay, you two and your Hallmark moments really suck." Alex wiped a tear in her eye. The two of them hugged, and Alex blew her nose with a tissue she grabbed from her backpack.

Anne, too, was trying to hide her tears. "Well, let's go complete your outfit." Once they paid for the clothes, they sat down at the food court. Anne ordered a garden wrap while Alex got a double cheeseburger. They were making idle chit-chat when Anne saw Mr. Dupel with who she assumed was his wife. She was very pregnant and equally as beautiful.

He escorted his wife to the two of them. "Ladies."

"Mr. Dupel," Anne greeted. Alex was in mid-bite as he approached. She just nodded as a greeting.

"This is my glowing wife, Veronica." He introduced her. "And our future baby girl, Elaina."

"That's a pretty name. Congratulations." Anne smiled at her.

"Thank you." She rubbed her stomach. "I feel like a house." She looked down at Alex's burger. "And one of those. Where did you get that?"

Alex pointed to the proper burger stand. "Right over there."

"Do you want one?" Veronica pulled out her wallet.

Mr. Dupel chuckled at his wife. "Extra pickles." He watched his wife walk away with pride. "What brings you ladies out?"

"Clothes shopping," Both Alex and Komptin both perked as they scanned the area.

"Alex still needs to finish her outfit." Anne looked around, trying to figure out what Alex was searching for.

"I saw that leather jacket store on the other end of the mall is having a sale." Mr. Dupel watched as his wife got their tray of food. He motioned to the table on the far end of the court. "I gotta go. Take care. See you Monday."

"He's a good one," Anne stated as she watched him join his wife. He was rubbing his wife's stomach. "You ever want kids?"

"I'm not able to," Alex continued to scan the area.

"The byproduct of being, you know..." Anne was afraid she had overstepped her boundaries.

Alex turned to Anne. "No, I had a hysterectomy. I had a problem with mechanics down there. They had to take them out."

"Alex, I'm sorry," Anne felt bad for bringing that up.

"Don't be." Alex continued to be distracted. "What do you say we go look at that leather store?" Alex's attention focused on the dark corner of the mall. She could have sworn she saw the shadow move. There was a small sense of the Dark, but she couldn't place it. It wasn't an Infiltrator sense; it was something else. It was a feeling she had sensed before.

CHAPTER FOUR

Alex opened the school's back entrance door, where Shawn was talking to one of the sophomore girls. The younger classmen seemed to be smitten with the tall king of the school. Alex met Shawn's eyes as he gave her a single wink with a smirk. Alex resisted the urge to smack him because she knew he started spreading it around that she fooled around with Donny.

Normally, these types of rumors wouldn't bother her, mainly because they were true. Something hit her that night besides an Infiltrator. "It's pretty bad if you can't make it with Alex Johnson." That one stung.

Alex saw Kale giving Anne a ride on his wheelchair down the hallway. She was sitting on his lap as he rolled towards the secret Lite Sentry. That brought a smile to Alex's face. Komptin was excited to see the two of them as well. Alex had to smile as Mr. Dupel stopped them to tell them that Anne could manage to walk down the hallway herself.

Alex approached her brother and his girlfriend. "Hey. Is Anne causing trouble again? Such a problem child."

Anne turned red from embarrassment. "I'm sorry again, Mr. Dupel."

Kale started to roll back to balance on the wheels of his mobile chair. "Sorry, just in a good mood." Kale swung around on his chair. "I got accepted to Chalice," he started to chant.

"Congratulations." Mr. Dupel prevented Kale from falling backward. "How about you try to make it there in one piece?"

"That's about twenty minutes from St. Michaels," Alex was thrilled that her brother would be close to her. She couldn't contain herself; she hugged him right there. "Best news I could get."

Alex turned to Anne, realizing she looked upset. "What's wrong?"

"It's just, I'm going to be in Arizona. Just reality is hitting me." Anne realized what time it was. "I have to get to the Student Council meeting." She grabbed Kale's hand before departing for her appointment.

"You know. It sucks when you find something you didn't even know you were looking for, but then get hit with the realization you're on a time limit." Kale watched Anne go into the classroom, where she was turning over the leadership to the next elected official.

Mr. Dupel put his hand on Kale's shoulder. "If it's meant to be, life will keep you together." He tapped his shoulder in support. "Now, roll onto class."

"Will do, Mr. Dupel." Mole met up with Dan as he helped guide him to his classroom. Dan's body language was one of excitement as he too was accepted to Chalice.

That left Alex and Mr. Dupel standing in the hallway. "Oh, that's right. I have something for you." Alex reached into her backpack. She handed him the card that Father Hanley gave her back at work. "They need to ask some questions."

"Hey, Alex!" A kid yelled. Alex turned to see a kid she recognized but didn't know his name. He was walking with Donny, and their laughter was no doubt directed at Alex. "When is it going to be my turn?" The group laughed as they headed down the hallway. Alex could hear one of them say they wanted a swing as well.

Mr. Dupel watched the boys head towards their classroom. Then he saw Alex, who had just closed her eyes and shaken her head. "Come on, Alex, perhaps you can help me answer some of these questions."

Alex sat across from Mr. Dupel as he turned on his computer. In awkward silence, she just sat in front of his desk. He put the card in front of his computer. Alex didn't know what he was doing. "Aren't you going to call?"

"I will, just thought we'd talk first." His kind eyes locked with Alex's. "Wanna tell me what that was all about?"

"Not really," Alex turned away from him.

Mr. Dupel got himself a cup of coffee. "I hear a lot in these halls; sometimes, the kids out there forget my office is even here. There's a lot said, rumors, untasteful bragging." He turned to Alex after getting his coffee.

"Can't be rumors if they're true," Alex was just loud enough for him to hear.

"You know Alex, you're probably the most confident young lady I've seen roam these halls. But there seems to be something else in your life missing; this can cause people to look for a quick fix to complete it. It can be drugs, alcohol, or even sex with multiple partners." He observed Alex's reaction. "They all have negative consequences if you abuse them to fill that need." He sat down on top of his desk in front of Alex. "There's something about you that is special. I can't put my finger on it, but you're destined to do great things."

Alex got a little embarrassed. "Thanks." She gathered her belongings. "I need to get to class. Are you going to call St. Michaels?"

"You have my word." He smiled at her as he raised his hand.

Alex stepped out of the guidance counselor's office feeling a little bit better about herself. She had about ten minutes before class started. She decided to grab a snack cake from the vending machine. Hayden's reflection was behind her. Alex opened her snack cake. The savory rush of sugar tasted so good. She turned around to see he still hadn't moved. "What's up, Hayden." Alex prayed he wasn't trying to get with her before the school year ended.

"I was wondering if you were able to get me that job at your church." Hayden stepped out of the way so Alex could get through.

"Thank you." Alex got out to the hallway with Hayden following her. "Let me ask you something: why do you want this job so much?"

"It looks good on a college resume," Hayden admitted.

"It's not the right reason to take the job. Are you Catholic?" Alex and Hayden continued down the hallway.

Hayden laughed, "Are you?"

"Got me on that one." Alex turned around as she felt that same weirdness of the Dark. Komptin himself felt it as well. It was so faint; it wasn't an Infiltrator, but something else. Then, as before, it seemed to disappear. The only thing she could think of it could be was a Demon, considering she still couldn't sense them unless they used their powers. The good news was that it wasn't Hayden. She didn't really want to kill one of her classmates, well, maybe one of them.

"Come on, Alex. I'm a hard worker, and I'm never late." Hayden started to give his qualifications. "Here, let me give you my phone number so you can at least introduce me."

Alex didn't really know how to get out of the situation. It's not like Hayden could go around killing Infiltrators in the middle of the night. "Fine." Alex just agreed to get out of this situation.

"Thanks, I owe you." Hayden went away with a spring in his step.

Alex laughed as she glanced down at Komptin. "Do you think he'd want the job if he knew what it entailed?" She playfully roughed up Komptin's head.

"Hey, Alex!" Alex lifted her eyes to see Donny with a group of guys coming down the hallway. One of them yelled, "Want to meet up this Friday?" He laughed with Donny.

Alex could feel her teeth clench, and her arms started to tingle. Komptin must have sensed it because he turned to Alex with a slight glow in his eyes. It was almost as if he was telling her to control herself. Alex closed her eyes to calm herself down. "I'm okay." She bent down to pet her companion.

Alex stood up to be met with a fist across the face. "I told your slut ass to stay away from him," Brooke screamed at her.

The punch really didn't have that much effect on Alex. It didn't even cause her to stagger–but it was enough to piss her off. Alex blocked another punch coming and swung Brooke into the lockers. Brooke's body slammed against the hollowed metal wall. Alex didn't even hesitate as she very easily threw Brooke to the other side of the hallway.

The crowd instantly gathered around the fight like sharks in the water, instigating it to go on. Alex drowned them out. Her vision was pinpointed on Brooke. The blonde girl barely had any time to put her hands up before Alex grabbed her by the throat. She put her fist up for a punch before Komptin jumped on Alex, knocking her down onto the cemented floor. The German Shepherd took a protective position over Alex, facing any potential threat. The dog turned to Brooke, growling before letting out a massive bark. The crowd immediately backed away once Komptin's growl seemed to echo through the hallways.

Mr. Pogolowski came in with another teacher. "What happened?"

Robbie stepped out of the crowd. "Brooke just punched Alex for no reason. Alex was just minding her own business when Brooke just sucker punched her."

"Stay away from him, you slut." Brooke spat towards Alex, but it landed on Komptin instead.

"Get her out of here," Mr. Pogolowski pointed to the principal's office. He faced Komptin with shaking hands. "It's okay, boy. I'm just going to help her up. Okay? Easy now."

"He won't hurt you," Alex got up to get to one knee. She tried to hide her tears of embarrassment and shame after cleaning up the spit off of Komptin.

Mr. Pogolowski turned to the group of students watching the show. "Go on, go to class before I put all of you in detention." The crowd immediately dispersed to their respective destinations, talking about how Alex never disappoints when it comes to fighting.

Alex hugged Komptin tightly as she cried. "Thank you," she whispered in his ear. She didn't want to let him go as she felt Mr. Pogolowski's hand on her shoulder.

"Alex." It was the first time he had ever called her by her first name. It was such a caring and strong tone. "Come on. Let's go."

***

The principal gave Alex the option to take an excused day off if she needed it. It was nice that she didn't call Alex's parents. She was considered an adult, so it was up to her if she wanted her parents notified. Technically, Alex could miss the rest of the year and be in no danger of not graduating. Alex didn't feel like going home, so she decided to take refuge in the church. For some reason, she didn't go to her office, as the congregation room felt like a safe haven.

The church was empty; it was a welcoming quiet. Father Hanley was secluded in his office. He didn't know Alex was in the building. The Lite Sentry sat in the front pew to stare at the stained-glass window. Her hand over her face in shame and fear.

"Alex?" Father Hanley came into the room. "Why aren't you in school?"

"I had a rough morning," Alex muffled through her hands. "Principal gave me an excused absence."

"What are you doing here?" The priest sat behind Alex in the wooden pew.

Alex turned back to the window. "Just felt right; safe."

"What happened?" Father Hanley leaned forward.

Alex couldn't really think how to explain what happened. "Some girl hit me because she thought I was sleeping with her boyfriend."

"No offense, but were you?" Father Hanley was worried about the answer.

Alex shook her head. "No, but I don't have the greatest reputation in the school, so I can see her point."

"I see," Father Hanley didn't know that about her. He got a phone call that he sent straight to voicemail. "Why did they send you home?"

"That fight activated my PTSD." Alex just sat there. "I needed to get away." Komptin got up and put his head on Alex's lap.

Father Hanley's phone went off again, he again sent it directly to voicemail. "Do you want to talk about it?"

Alex shook her head. "Nope."

Father Hanley was about to push the issue, but then he got a text message on his phone. "Oh, man."

Alex saw the stress on the priest's face. "Are you okay?"

"Remember that confession I told you about the other day?" He typed something on his phone.

"Yes," Alex started to scratch her dog's ears.

"Seems like there is more to the story. I have to go." Father Hanley stopped himself. "Are you going to be okay?"

"I'll be fine," she smiled. "Really, I'm fine."

The priest nodded before he got up to leave. "I'll be back in a bit if you want to talk."

Alex waved bye to him. The Lite Sentry waited a bit before she went to the kitchen to grab a glass with ice. She poured her Apollo Energy Drink before heading back up to the congregation room. She didn't know how long she sat there, but it was long enough for the condensation to build up around the glass.

"What is on your mind, Alexandria?" A calming voice came from behind her.

Alex turned around to see Celestial sitting down with Ariel and Devine proudly standing behind her. "I got into a fight at school today."

"Yes," Celestial gave her Lite Sentry a caring mother's look. "Are you hurt?"

"No," Alex didn't understand that question. It didn't hardly affect her. "I got scared."

The blonde angel went in front of Alex. "What caused your fear?"

Alex was ashamed, and she didn't want to answer. "I could have killed her. Komptin saved me from making a horrible mistake. I didn't even think about what would have happened if I punched someone normal."

"Where did that anger stem from? What you need to worry about, Alexandria, is not only the cause of anger, but the directional method you use to release it. Are you angry at her, at the group of boys, or yourself?"

Alex thought about it for a bit. "I guess there is no black-and-white answer, is there? I'm responsible for my actions that caused my reputation. Brooke didn't handle her fears in the best manner, and the boys are just jackasses."

Celestial smirked. "Not all boys make the same mistakes. There are some out there with truly pure hearts."

Alex started to fight back her emotions. "I almost killed her. I didn't even think twice about it. I guess I'm just not cut out for being a Sentry." Alex thought about it.

"That is the most stupid thing…" Devine finally had enough.

Ariel finished her thought, "…that we have ever heard you say."

"…and there has been a lot," they both spoke with conviction.

The two came to make sure they were seen in front of Alex. Ariel was the first to speak. "He was the One who asked you, because He saw what is in you..."

Devine came up to her and pointed directly at her chest. "...you Alexandria Johnson, accepted this responsibility, if you do not think you are worth it..."

"Then you slander His name with blunder." Ariel pointed to the sun shining in the yellow circle in the stained-glass window. "Do you want to stand before Him with that acquisition?"

"Then you truly are." There was a pause as they looked at each other, and then they turned back to her. "Stupid."

Celestial guided herself in between the Guardians of the Conduit. "Alexandria," she was trying to hide the humor she found in her guardians. "I believe what they are saying is..." She knelt down to Alex's eye level. Alex started to stand to prevent the angel from kneeling in front of her. Celestial put her hand on her shoulder, as if telling her not to move. "...you are learning. Even the most elite of us still make mistakes." Celestial glanced over to her Guardians. "The important item to take away is that you learn." The elegant blonde angel stood up. "Someday, you will have to fight, man or woman, who have not been infiltrated; you will learn to control your power." She leaned over and kissed her on top of her head. She generated a treat from her hand to feed to Komptin before she left, escorted by her guardians.

CHAPTER FIVE

Alex couldn't wait to move out of her parent's house. Not because of the rules, curfew, or the fact she had to sneak out on nights she hunted. It was because the nights she didn't stalk the Dark, she just laid her bed, staring at the ceiling. Her phone could only provide only so much amusement for so long. The TV would wake her parents up, so she just stared at the ceiling.

Komptin was at the foot of her bed, comforted by lying on her feet. Sometimes, she thought it was because he didn't want her to sneak out without him. Although she would hate to admit it, having him with her was a nice sense of security. She could not forget the fact he saved her from making a terrible mistake.

Alex just stared out the window. Osiah's star, which only beings of the Lite could witness, was shining bright–how she missed him. He was one of those people that came into her life that she instantly connected with. She was sorry it was so short-lived.

Some of the training sessions he gave were quite painful. He drew blood on her multiple times. The first time she started to bleed from the nose, he told her that it was the first of many. Fortunately, the Lite would ensure she had plenty to spill.

She moved back to stare at the ceiling. Komptin opened one eye to see what was going on. "Sorry." He quickly went back to bed. There was a welcome packet from St. Michaels that she finally decided to read. It was the basic school stuff; nothing really caught her attention, except the school uniforms. She didn't really understand why…then, her thought was interrupted.

She and Komptin both looked to the window as the staleness of the air filled their senses. They both flashed their eyes towards the window. Alex didn't really want to go hunting this late, but that was way too close. She had about six hours before she had to go to school, and her parents would be up in about two hours. She was going to have to wait. This irritated Alex; she had such an urge to get out there, but there was no way she wouldn't get caught if she went. All morning, Alex kept on thinking about the Infiltration that took place last night. She kept tapping on her coffee cup and looking at the woods from the bench swing. Her dad joined her in his bathrobe.

He just stared ahead at the woods. "Thinking of the future?"

"You could say that." Alex continued her watchful eye on the forest, knowing she was going to be going hunting on this night.

"You think your future is in those trees?" Her dad put his arm around his little girl.

Alex accepted the cuddle. She placed her head on her father's shoulder. They just sat and stared at the forest. A small fawn came out of the woods with her mother not far behind. Alex was glad to see the skittish animal. That meant the Dark wasn't near the house.

Her mom came out with two cups of coffee. She handed one to her husband before she sat next to her daughter. Alex became the center of her parent's sandwich, and she loved it. The two of them just sat there, enjoying the morning. Alex teared up, as she knew this was probably going to be the last time she would have a moment like this.

***

Alex stared at the school from the outside of her car in the parking lot. This was the last week of school, and after this week, Alex would no longer be roaming these halls. It was bittersweet. On one end, she was about to start her life– her own life. On the other, she now had a lifetime of battling the Dark ahead of her. Which was fine. She was glad to do it, but there were times she wondered what she had sacrificed.

"Looks different, doesn't it," Kale rolled up in his chair.

"It does," Alex watched as the younger classmen started their way into the building. "Where's Anne?"

"She had to skip the morning. Some important college meeting." Mole started rolling up to the school with Alex and Komptin beside him.

"How was your night?" Alex offered him half her breakfast sandwich.

He kindly denied it as he pulled out a banana and yogurt. "Couldn't sleep."

"Me either," Alex watched as she saw Mr. Dupel get out of his car. "Looks like he didn't sleep either." The guidance counselor was obviously tired as he went into the school, not saying a word to anyone.

"That doesn't seem like him," Mole dumped some granola in his yogurt. "Anne got me hooked on this. The secret is to add a couple of chocolate chips to it. Doesn't that sound good?"

"No, it doesn't," Alex was staring off at the school.

"Well, it is." Mole took in a spoonful of yogurt.

Alex looked down at Mole, eating his yogurt. "What? No, I'm not talking about the yogurt, you big ape." Alex went behind Mole to push him to the school so he could eat. "Come on, let's get to class." Alex was worried about Mr. Dupel being infiltrated, but she just figured that he probably didn't get much sleep because his wife was so close to giving birth.

Inside the school, it hit Alex like a wall of stale stench. She was amazed no one noticed it. There was no doubt about it. The Dark was here. Granted, she still couldn't hone her senses of the Demon unless they used their power. Osiah had told her that it would come with time. One day, she could look into someone's eyes and tell they were a Demon. But until she learned how to do that, she had to wait until they used their power. That made it much more difficult. It still didn't prevent her from investigating.

Alex was on her way to Mythology to turn in her books. There was no reason for her to be here. She had already graduated. Mainly, the last week was all about transitioning. Mole had to take his last exam this morning. Then, they had Senior

Assembly to go over graduation practice. On her way, she saw Mr. Dupel heading towards his office.

He had an angry aurora to him. There were some kids goofing around, but he didn't stop them; he just kept going. Almost like he didn't care. Alex saw that Komptin was on edge. He sensed something he didn't like. Alex was beyond worried. What if he accepted Infiltration? But why would he? He was one of the nice ones. The fact that Alex might have to dispose of him didn't really make her feel all that great.

All day at school, Alex was trying to find a reason to go see Mr. Dupel. The principal told her that he took a personal day. Alex just assumed that his wife must be getting close to delivering the baby. But if he took a personal day for that, then that's a good chance he's not a Demon. There were too many unanswered questions.

All the students were in their classrooms, but the secret Lite Sentry. Alex quietly roamed the hallways of the school. It was quiet. The only sounds were faint lectures from some of the classrooms. Some classrooms were energetic, and some were just flat-out awful. Although, it was funny to Alex that she remembered some of the same lectures. Alex made it to the third floor; near the end of the hallways was the guidance counselor's office.

The light was off, and Alex couldn't hear anything. The door was obviously locked; it really was no matter. She very easily just turned the knob with her strength, breaking the lock. She quickly glanced around to make sure no one saw her. The

Lite Sentry snuck into the office, with Komptin staying by the door as a lookout. Alex focused on anything to prove Mr. Dupel wasn't infiltrated.

His office was pretty basic. There was a picture of him and his wife at a ski resort, almost as if it was a professional photo shoot. There was another picture of her in a dress on the beach as the sun was setting. Alex picked up the photo. This one was no doubt taken by a professional. Alex opened an album on his shelf. It was all these specialized photo shoots of his wife. On some of the pages were some catalog photos of her modeling dresses. Near the end of the album was a letter from his wife. It read how proud she was of him. She even kissed the letter, leaving a mark on the paper.

"No, I refuse to think he is infiltrated." Alex put the album back. She sat down at his desk, going through some of the drawers. Komptin turned to Alex and flashed his eyes. That weird sense of the Dark came again. It didn't feel like an Infiltrator, but it was definitely Dark. Then, it was gone just as fast as it came. Alex continued to search, but then a silhouette of a person approached the door. Alex froze. The shadow of the person just froze in front of the door. It seemed like an eternity before it moved. Then, the figure just walked away.

Alex was almost in fear of whoever, or whatever, it was; it must have sensed her Lite. A couple of moments passed to make sure it didn't come back. As a last-ditch effort, she tried to open his main desk drawer. It was locked. There didn't seem to be any key around, but luckily, Alex didn't really need it. She easily pried open the drawer with her hand. There wasn't really much in there. Perhaps a couple of dollars in change, a really nice pen, markers, a pamphlet on parenthood, cough drops, and some other office supplies. Although, she did find his checkbook.

She opened it up to see that the background of the checks was some college logo, probably from where he went to school. She took out her phone to take a picture of his address. "Come on, Komptin. We're just going to make sure tonight." She carefully opened the office door to make sure no one was around. There was that quick sense of something Dark, but as before, it quickly vanished.

***

It was dark out as Alex sat in her car with Komptin sitting upright in the back seat. His head poked in between the two front seats. Alex was scratching her dog's head as she was texting Anne and Kale. The two of them were at Anne's house watching a movie. Alex liked that. They seemed so happy together.

This surveillance was going nowhere. There wasn't any sense of the Dark. Alex was starting to get nervous about looking like a stalker sitting in the car on the street. Mr. Dupel's house was fancy for a teacher's salary. It must have been paid for with his wife's modeling money. Alex reached around to scratch Komptin behind the ears. "This is stupid. There is no hard evidence that he's infiltrated."

The garage door opened, and Mr. Dupel came out. Alex waited a bit before she started the car to follow him. She stayed her distance but still kept him in sight. She followed him out of town, past Westington and about ten miles out towards the woods. "Where the hell is he going?" Alex asked Komptin. "Why am I asking you?" She roughed up his head a bit. The two hunters continued to follow him, Anne he turned down the back road to go deep into the forest.

She shut the lights off to turn down the road to follow him undetected. The privilege of being a Lite Sentry gave her the ability to see in the dark easily. She found a spot to park the car off the road. She had been in this area before; her dad took her here to go fishing. There was a small lake down one of these roads where you could only use a canoe or kayak.

Alex continued down the unlit road. There were sounds of night animals calling out, but other than that, there were no sounds. There were some fresh car tracks going to the part of the woods next to the lake. "Go, secure around the lake." She motioned to Komptin. Alex continued to move forward, where there was a small cabin. Mr. Dupel's car was parked in front of it. The cabin was modern and must have been expensive. She peeked in the window where Mr. Dupel was reading something on his phone. He was annoyed when he started to shut everything off.

Alex was fed up with trying to put this together. It was just the two of them. She wanted to know right here and now if he was a Demon. She waited until he came out of the cabin before she said, "Mr.

Dupel." Alex leaned on his car to prevent him from leaving.

"Jesus, Alex. What are you doing here?" He scanned the area around him.

"Really, just to talk." She studied him intensely. "Are you really who you say you are?"

Mr. Dupel laughed. "What?" He double-checked the door. Then he stared towards his car, but yet still kept his distance.

Alex was about to leave until she got a sense of the Dark. Komptin was still off in the woods. There was a chance he still may have been a Demon. Alex needed to make sure. "Mr. Dupel, there's something I need to do, but it makes me scared of the future."

"It's called graduation, Alex. Everyone goes through it." Mr. Dupel put his hands in his pockets. "But following me to my cabin is highly inappropriate. You're putting me in a very awkward situation."

"Sorry, I just needed to make sure. You ever know the answer but just need to verify to ease your mind?" Alex shifted herself on the car. There was a faint sense of the Dark around, but nothing alarming.

"I get it." Mr. Dupel put his phone in his pocket. "But again, highly inappropriate to follow me out here."

"Sorry," Alex just moved her eyes back and forth to see if anything was going to attack her. "I guess what I'm looking for isn't here. I'll see you tomorrow." Then Alex felt that weird sense of the Dark. She couldn't place it. It was so faint, so distinctive. She closed her eyes to see if she could get a better grasp on it.

The next thing she felt was a pair of lips on hers. Her body was pushed up against the car, and she felt of an adult hand sliding up the outside of her shirt. She pushed Mr. Dupel off of her. "What the hell are you doing?!"

"Stop playing these games with me, Alex. I know you've wanted this for some time." Mr. Dupel tried to be gentle as he grabbed her face. "The whole school knows how free-spirited you are to live the moment. Let's make our moment work for us." He opened his mouth to kiss her again.

Alex put her hand up to block the kiss. "Ah, no. There is a really big misunderstanding going on here. Plus, you're married, with a kid on the way."

"She'll never know, trust me. Come on, stop teasing. Why else would you follow me to the woods? Let me make you feel like the special woman you are." He went in for a kiss.

"No," Alex flat-out said.

"You won't regret it." Mr. Dupel got a little forceful as he put his arms on each side of Alex, entrapping her against the car.

Alex very easily pushed his arms out of the way and slammed his head onto the car. "Oh my God! I can't believe this!" She whistled as loud as she could. "Komptin, we're leaving!"

"Come on, Alex. Don't be afraid. We're just two adults, who just have a need for an unforgettable night together." Mr. Dupel rubbed his head.

"You take one more step towards me, and I swear to God, I will show you something you will never forget." Alex put up her hands in a defensive position.

"Really, Alex?" Mr. Dupel saw that she meant it. "I'm not going to assault you. I'm not a rapist. I'm just a person who sees how beautiful you are."

Alex put her arms down. For a quick second, she thought about taking him on his seductive offer, but then shook it off. "I'm leaving."

"Alex," Mr. Dupel started to come towards her.

Komptin charged out of the woods to get in between the two of them. Mr. Dupel watched as Alex talked to herself and went back to her car. The German Shepherd stood in an attack position with his growling head down. Komptin eyed the man, as if almost daring him to take one more step towards Alex. With a single whistle from Alex, Komptin joined Alex by her side. The two of them disappeared into the thickness of the forest.

CHAPTER SIX

Even without the power of the Lite to keep her up at night, Alex didn't think she would have been able to sleep. It just disgusted her what Mr. Dupel did. With much confusion, Alex got up to go to school. She sat in the parking lot, debating on what she was going to do. There was no doubt what he did was wrong, but technically, she was eighteen and an adult. Plus, she only had three days left of school; besides betraying his wife, what harm did Mr. Dupel actually do?

He was a little forceful but didn't push himself onto her. Would it be worth bringing it up to the administration? More so, would they believe her? A knock on the window caused Alex to jump a bit. She rolled down the window to Mole and Anne. "What's up?"

"Coming to school?" Mole was eye-level with her from sitting in his chair.

Alex rolled up her window before opening the door. "I guess if I have to." Anne looked like she had something on her mind. "What's with you?"

"I had a very long talk with my parents last night." Anne rubbed her eyes. "I didn't get much sleep."

Mole tilted his head back to see his girlfriend. "Everything okay?"

"I will find out today, hopefully." Anne rubbed his shoulders before giving him a kiss on the cheek.

"Watch the PDA." Mr. Dupel yelled from across the parking lot.

"You got it, Mr. D," Mole waved to him.

Alex just got disgusted by the sight of him. "Let's get this over with; I can't wait to get the hell out of this building."

Mole got dropped off at his class to turn in his books while Alex and Anne continued down the halls before their mandatory life transitioning seminar in the gym. "You going to tell me what's going on with you?" Alex tried to pry it out of her good friend.

Anne just kept facing the ground. "I'm going to make a decision, life-altering."

"I know the feeling," Alex rubbed her friend's back. "What's the decision?"

"It's not a smart one," Anne held her stomach with her arms.

Alex dragged Anne into the school cafeteria. It was just the two of them sitting in the room. The kitchen staff was prepping lunch for the junior classmen. "Now you have my attention. What foolish mistake is Anne McClure going to make?" Alex gave her a little tease.

Anne scanned the area almost to make sure no one was listening. Almost like she couldn't believe she was about to say the words. "I'm not going to Arizona State."

Alex's eyes got big. "What? Why?"

Anne just got a guilty smirk on her face. "I want to be with Kale."

"Are you pregnant?" For some reason, that was the first thing that came to her mind.

Anne laughed, "No." She sat down on the cafeteria chair. "I woke up yesterday morning with the feeling that I was up all night talking to someone. I can't explain it, but when I opened my eyes, my future was Kale."

"You're giving up going to Arizona State, to be with Mole?" Alex didn't know what to say. "Look, I love Mole to death, but what you are doing is…pretty dumb, Anne."

Anne's face knew Alex was right. "That's what my father said. But when you get a feeling like this, you have to go with it. All my life, I never took chances, always prepped, always studied… always took the safe route that I planned beforehand; then, one fateful night, I took a chance on Kale Moler, and it was the best decision I have ever made."

"What was your parents' final word on it?" Alex watched Komptin lay down on the floor. Alex was sitting on top of the table to talk to Anne.

"Shockingly, they supported the decision." Anne got up from the chair. "Kale just texted me. We are going to meet up with our parents for lunch. Wanna come?"

"No, this is all you. Are you going to tell Kale?"

Anne laughed, "On our way to lunch."

"Good luck with that."

***

Alex stayed behind in the cafeteria; she had a couple of minutes before she had to turn her books to her second-period government class. She moved to sit on the chair as she put her feet up on the table.

She decided to pull out her welcome packet to St. Michaels to start seeing what she'd gotten into. The principal stopped as she was passing by. She told her to put her feet down before heading back to wherever she was going.

Alex saw that it was time to head to turn in her book anyway. The hallways were empty with the anticipation of excited kids to be that much closer to the end of the school year. Alex turned the corner and got hit with that weird sense of the Dark again. Even Komptin flashed his eyes to confirm he felt it as well. Alex stopped in her tracks, and it was gone.

Perhaps it was a Demon. Alex was just getting more irritated. This in and out of the Dark was starting to really get under her skin. She stood in one place for a bit to see if she could sense it, but there was nothing. Alex had no idea what it could be. There was nothing she could do about it, so she continued to move ahead with her day.

Just as she was about to leave, she and Komptin heard something coming from the women's bathroom. It almost sounded like whimpering. Alex motioned for Komptin to stay by the door as she went in. She slowly peeked into the restroom, where there was a student sitting on the floor with her head in between her knees, crying. "Hey, you okay?"

The woman lifted her head, and Alex saw it was Brooke in full-out tears. It looked like she had been crying for a while, like it was almost sadness mixed with fear. She closed her eyes in utter fear as she asked Alex in between her tears, "Did you sleep with him? Because I did."

Alex knelt down to her level, putting her hand on Brooke's knee as a sign of compassion. "Brooke, there is nothing going on between me and Hayden. Really, he was just asking me about the job at the church. And tell you the truth, I think he's got it really bad for you." She warmly smiled at the distraught person before her.

That brought Brooke to more tears. "Oh God." She was now full-out crying.

"Brooke, what's going on?" Alex was trying to calm her down.

"I'm, I'm pregnant." She could barely get out.

Alex tried not to act shocked. "Brooke, that's not a bad thing. Granted, the timing isn't the greatest, but it will be okay. It will be rough, but you will make a great mom. I don't think Hayden is the type of person that would abandon the mother of his child."

Brooke lifted her head up. "He's not the father."

"Oh," Alex felt stupid. She didn't know what to do. "Who is?"

"Mr. Dupel." The blonde woman before her slowly said.

"What?" Alex was taken back a bit. She stood up in shock, putting it all together, but then knelt back down.

Brooke had a river of tears flowing down her face. "He told me there was something special about me. He never met a woman like me."

Alex swallowed hard. "We need to go to the principal."

Brooke shook her head. "I can't. My parents don't even know." Brooke grabbed Alex by the shirt with scared conviction in her eyes. "Promise me you won't say anything." She pulled Alex in closer to her. "Promise me."

"Okay, okay, Brooke." Alex slowly removed Brooke's hands from her clothes. Alex sat down next to Brooke on the floor. "So, what are you going to do?"

Brooke wiped her nose. "I don't know."

Then Brooke did something that Alex wasn't expecting. She put her head on Alex's shoulder. Alex put her arm around Brooke to comfort her. "No matter what happens, Brooke, you will have support." Alex moved her eyes around as they started to glow. There was Dark around, but Alex couldn't find it. It was a lot stronger than she felt before, but it wasn't an Infiltrator. Komptin came into the bathroom, almost in guard mode. He knew the Dark was in here. But why couldn't Alex see it?

Brooke just stared forward, almost in fear. "Sometimes my thoughts scare me the most, Alex." The young woman held her stomach. "My life is ruined."

"No, Brooke. It's just going in a different direction." Alex continued to scan the bathroom. For a second, she thought she saw something move into the shadows of the corner of the bathroom, but it must have been her imagination.

"I need to go." Brooke got up and then helped Alex off the floor. "I'm sorry for treating you like shit, Alex. I figured you were trying to sleep with Mr. Dupel. I thought Mr. Dupel and I were something special together. Can you forgive me?"

"Of course." Alex hugged Brooke. The two of them came out of the bathroom where Mr. Dupel had just turned the corner to see the two of them. Alex pushed Brooke in the opposite direction. "Go, Brooke. Go on."

Mr. Dupel calmly watched Brooke down the hall. Then he moved his eyes down to the young woman, staring directly into his eyes. "She is a very disturbed young lady, even delusional."

"You're an asshole," Alex said in her most calm voice.

"And you haven't graduated yet, Ms. Johnson," Mr. Dupel threatened.

"Fine. Let's go talk to the principal, right now." Alex stood her ground, not backing down. "I'm sure there is plenty we can talk about." Alex searched into his eyes, trying to sense some form of Dark in him.

Mr. Dupel didn't even change his expression. "I can talk to people as well. I understand Anne is dating your brother. They look good together."

Alex lost her confident look. "Okay, and?"

"Anne came to me this morning; she'll need my signature for her application to attend that college near her crippled boyfriend." Mr. Dupel checked his watch. "I'm just saying."

Before he looked up, Alex grabbed him and shoved him into the wall. "Don't you dare."

"Let go of me." Mr. Dupel removed her hands from his clothes. He gently rubbed his fingers over her hands. Alex pulled them back, shivering. It was so disgusting. She wiped her hands on her clothes. Alex searched in his eyes again, but there was no Dark. She just shook her head in shock. "Now, if you will excuse me, Alex. I have some phone calls to make."

***

The church was a calming quiet. It was much needed before her hunt tonight. Luckily, her parents were going out of town tonight for some lawyer thing and wouldn't be back until tomorrow night. She sat back in the office in the upstairs of the church. Her feet were up on her desk as she watched Osiah's star staring back at her. It was as if he was giving her advice.

"Does he speak to you?" Father Hanley leaned on the doorway of her office.

"I like to think so," Alex motioned for him to come in. Father Hanley sat down in the brown leather chair next to Alex's desk. "I like to think I make Him proud."

"You're not Catholic, are you?" Father Hanley had bags under his eyes as if he was stressed.

Alex shook her head. "Does that bother you?"

Father Hanley smiled. "Bother, no. Confuse, maybe."

"I'm an open book, padre." Alex refilled her glass with her open can of Apollo energy drink.

"I got a call from Father Carl Gray."

"Don't even know who that is," Alex continued to stare out the window.

Father Hanley wiped his face. "You will. He's the Dean of St. Michaels."

Alex didn't like where this was going. "And?"

"Apparently, he got a phone call from your school. They talked about multiple fights, being promiscuous, and not complying with rules and regulations. And that he should think twice about letting you attend." Father Hanley was getting uncomfortable with this conversation.

"That son of a..." Alex took her feet down off her desk. She was upset, and she ended up pacing a bit as Komptin watched her. She stopped at the window to stare in the direction of the school.

"Before I proceed with what I'm going to do, I need to know if any of it is true." Father Hanley stared at her. "Don't lie to me, especially in His house."

Alex was shocked at his serious tone. "I'm not afraid to bleed, and I'm no stranger to a man's touch." She turned to see his reaction.

Father Hanley nodded. "Thank you." He got up from his chair.

"What are you going to do?" Alex asked him.

Father Hanley turned to Alex. "Everything within the confines of my vows." He left the office to head downstairs.

Alex just watched him leave. She didn't know what that meant. What was going to happen to her now? What will the Council do? She turned to the window; for some reason, it got darker over the town.

CHAPTER SEVEN

Last night's hunt was a complete bust. It might have been a blessing in disguise, though. Alex couldn't think of anything but her college enrollment being in danger. It wasn't the mere fact that she wanted to wear a Catholic school uniform for four years. It was something different; she found herself caring about what the Council thought of her. It was weird. She normally didn't care what people's impression of Alexandria Johnson. However, a bunch of old guys in a foreign country had her concerned.

She was standing over the kitchen sink for breakfast, eating a bowl of sugary cereal with a bear on it. The marshmallows still had a crunch to them, mixed with a soft layer of milk. Komptin was outside, walking around the yard. There was no Dark around. Even the Dark knew not to go after Alex's family. Then, a whole new level of vengeance would be instigated. Alex just thought he liked to be alone once in a while. Alex watched her dog play with a baby deer as the fawn's mother ate her mom's shrubbery.

Alex got a text from her dad, who assured her that they would be home for her graduation on Friday. Alex tipped the bowl to her mouth to finish off her milk. She rinsed the bowl before putting it in the dishwasher. There was still no message from Father Hanley but there was one from Mole. He wanted to see if she could meet up for breakfast.

Alex hurried to the diner to meet her brother. This diner had the fluffiest stack of pancakes with whipped cream and strawberries. She was still hungry even though she had a bowl of cereal this morning. Mole ordered an egg-white omelet with a bowl of fruit. Alex felt Komptin underneath the table on her feet. It felt so warm and secure. "Weird that we don't have to be in school anymore?"

"It is," Mole wiped his mouth before drinking his orange juice. "What's on your mind? You look a little distant?"

"I had a rough day yesterday." Alex picked a strawberry seed out of her teeth.

"Anne dropped a bomb on me yesterday." Mole just came out with the reason he wanted to meet.

Alex tried to play it off like she didn't know. "Is she pregnant?"

"No," he shook his head out of disbelief. "She switched colleges to be close to me." Alex failed to act shocked. "You knew?"

"She told me." Alex took a sip of her coffee. It was really bitter, not that good. "How do you feel about it?"

"I was all excited at first, but then fear took over," Kale sliced into his omelet. The molten lava of cheese just poured out.

"Fear, from what?"

Mole looked around to make sure no one was listening. "What if I become the reason, she ruins her life?"

"You actually think Anne McClure has only one shot at a happy life?" Alex quietly yelled at him.

"Well, no." Mole sat there for a minute to think about it.

"You know what makes her happy? You, you big ape." Alex pointed in his direction.

"What if we break up?" Mole had a hard time pushing those words out. "Losing her is not something I can handle."

Alex went back to eating her breakfast. "Then you break up. Move on with life. It's stupid not to try something because of the fear of being happy. Who would do that?"

"I guess you're right. We have a chance of a real good thing here. I'm going to make this work." Mole smiled at the thought of a life with Anne.

"Good, plus all three of us can still be together." Alex was pleased at that thought, but then she realized that she might not be there. Her future was still in jeopardy. She checked her phone again. There was still no message from Father Hanley.

***

Alex parked her car in the back lot of the church. The music was vibrating the car; anything to try to get herself in a better mood. There was no sign of Father Hanley's car, and it wasn't parked out front, which probably meant he wasn't at the church. Alex got out of the car to a blast of that weird sensation of the Dark. Komptin was not immune to the staleness in the air.

Alex slammed her hands on the roof of her car. "That's it." Alex bee-lined it to the woods behind the church. She stepped off the property, and her eyes instantly glowed neon blue. "I'm right here, you chicken-shit, motherf–" Alex was about to finish her sentence when Komptin barked at a pair of red glowing floating in a tree in the distance. The eyes just stared at her. Alex motioned to it as if asking what it was waiting for. The eyes just flashed at her before taking off into the thickness of the forest.

Alex waited for a bit before she went into the church. Komptin stayed loyally by her side. The church was quiet. Alex scouted through the church, trying to see if anyone was around, but it seemed empty. Alex poked her head into Father Hanley's office. "Father?" But there was no one there. His phone rang, and for some reason, she picked it up. "Father Hanley's office."

A man with a thick Italian accent was on the other end of the phone. "Father Hanley, per favore."

Alex tightened her lip as she moved her body out of anger, kicking herself for answering the phone with the Council on the other end. "He's not in."

"Is this Ms. Johnson?" The man on the other end asked.

"Yah," Alex tightened up. She could hear some muffled Italian as the man on the other end was talking to someone. It seemed to last forever.

"We will talk later, arrivederci." The man hung up the phone.

Alex just heard the dial tone. "Later." She took a look at the receiver end of the phone before hanging up. She knew right then: she was getting denied her college. Now the Council would be more willing to send her all over the world to battle the Dark. She is going to have to leave all that she cared for behind. If she was in school, she'd be locked in one place for four years: with her brother and his girlfriend. Now, it was all in jeopardy.

Alex went upstairs to her office. She liked having her own little getaway in the building. She felt as if it was her oasis. Komptin went straight to his spot underneath the window. Alex picked up her picture of Osiah with Komptin. Alex took this self-portrait with each other after a training session. Alex remembered that rough night.

The woods were a lot darker than usual. Alex could see movement up ahead. It was just a light movement of leaves. Alex moved with elegant speed as she circled around to pounce on her prey. She made it around to see the creature move about. The wind was about to shift, giving up her position. She jumped on her victim's back, putting her blade around Komptin's neck. "Got you." She kissed him on top of his head. Komptin bucked her off, sending her flying into the air and crashing onto the forest floor. The massive gargoyle placed his enormous claws on Alex's shoulders. She couldn't budge. Komptin started to drown her with licks. "Okay, okay, I give."

A whistle came from the woods. Komptin jumped off Alex and joined Osiah at his side. The two of them looked at each other as they approached Alex. "You did good." The tall man with an orange and gray beard mixture approached the young Sentry.

"Thanks. I'm a total badass." Alex laughed. She extended her hand, but Osiah didn't offer to help her up. "Thanks for the help." Alex brushed herself off. She saw Osiah pacing back and forth a bit as if he was debating on something. Komptin took off into the woods as if something spooked him. "Where's he going?" Osiah didn't say anything. Alex just shrugged it off. Alex came up by Osiah. "I think we are going to put some serious fear into the Dark."

Osiah spun around, hitting her on the side of the head with the back of his fist. "Do you think you could actually put fear into the Dark, you pitiful excuse for a Sentry." He ran up to her and kicked her on the side. It sent her flying into a tree. Alex tried to defend herself against his unprovoked attack, but there was nothing she could do to prevent his assault; his punches kept on getting through. He picked her up and slammed her on the ground. "Give your allegiance to the Dark, and I'll let you live." Osiah's eyes were glowing bright purple as he put his hands around her neck. He clutched her throat before starting to squeeze.

"Bite me, you piece of–" Alex tried to push out, but Osiah's grip just tightened. She was starting to get weaker and weaker. The blackness was starting to take over her eyesight. How could he betray her? How could Osiah betray Celestial like this? These were questions that Alex wasn't going to be able to get answered, as she was about to come face to face with death.

Osiah let go of his grip around Alex's throat. Alex was slowly getting her vision back. "Are you okay?" He put his hand on her shoulder.

Alex smacked his hand away. "Fu–"

Osiah put his colossal hand over her mouth. "Tell me what you felt?"

"You're telling me this was a lesson?" Alex was furious. She was waiting for an answer, but her mentor just stared at her. "I thought I was going to die," Alex admitted, but still a little on guard.

Komptin came out from the thickened brush to join Osiah. The two of them stared at Alex. "Don't ever forget that feeling. That feeling is going to save your life. The minute you get relaxed, that is the day you die." Osiah pulled out his flask, and his hands shook as he tipped the metal container with his shaking hands to his mouth. It was almost like he didn't want to teach that lesson.

After that reality check, they all went for a walk. They discussed some pointers for fighting Infiltrators and the difference of combating Demons. The group of them stopped at a rock face, where she took a picture of the three of them.

"The old caretaker?" Father Hanley's voice interrupted Alex's trip down memory lane.

Alex nodded. "He saved my life." She put the picture down. Then, she went to sit on her desk. "You don't look good."

"Stressful day." Father Hanley leaned on the door.

"The Council called for you." Alex nonchalantly gave him the message from earlier.

Father Hanley looked at her with confusion. "What council?"

Alex forgot that Father Hanley didn't know anything about the Council of Religions. Then why did they call? "I got a phone call from a man with an Italian accent."

"Yes, he called my cell." Father Hanley acted as if he did not enjoy that phone conversation. "Look, Alex. I'm going to be frank. It's not looking good."

"This Dean of Education at St. Michaels is adamant that he doesn't want you there." Father Hanley started to lay out all the cards on the table.

"Is it because of my reputation?"

"Confirmed by a member of the administration staff at your school. That, mixed with your GPA, it's not a good cocktail." Father Hanley tried to be comforting.

"Thanks for being honest." Alex looked up to the ceiling out of frustration.

"What are you going to do? You can try to get into another school during the winter semester." The priest was trying to be upbeat.

"I don't know. I have a feeling I'm going to be bouncing around a lot." Alex fought back her tears. "I can't believe one piece of –" Alex stopped herself from cussing in front of Father Hanley. "...one vindictive man could have such power to ruin someone's life."

Father Hanley came up to Alex. "Don't lose faith. There is probably more to the story than you know." He tapped her on the shoulders.

"Well, my last day of school is tomorrow, so unless you have a miracle in your pocket, I'm pretty much screwed." All Alex could think of was that the Council wolfs be sending her all over the place.

"Keep your faith." He pointed to her heart before he left for the night.

"Keep your faith; keep your faith," Alex kept on saying to herself in a sarcastic tone. She didn't realize how long she was saying that until she walked into the congregation room. She stopped in her tracks as she looked at the stained-glass window. "Sorry." Guilt filled Alex as she knew deep down Father Hanley was right. She did need to keep faith. Alex got a text from Mole telling her to meet her at the football field tonight at ten.

***

It was nice to laugh with the group again. Dan was pushing Mole around the football field as Robbie threw the ball to Mole. "Touchdown!" Dan yelled as he twirled his friend around in his wheelchair.

Anne and Alex were sitting on a blanket on the field. Anne yelled, "Way to go, baby!"

Robbie started to tease Mole. "Dude, that cheerleader over there's got it bad for you."

"Think I have a chance?" Mole playfully winked at Anne.

Dan peeked over at Anne. "Nope. Looks like she has standards and taste." He rubbed his friend's head.

The graduating guys came to the blanket to join the two girls. Mole winced as he lifted himself out of the chair to sit down next to Anne. He lay down on the ground while Anne held him in her arms. He enjoyed her soft hand caressing his hair with her soft fingers.

Alex smiled at the genuine care they had for each other. "Well, after tomorrow. We're done."

"Thank God," Robbie told them. "No offense, but I need to get out of this town."

"I get it," Dan agreed. "Hasn't been the easiest end of our senior year."

"Where'd you end up anyway?" Robbie zipped up his University of Minnesota jacket.

Mole answered for Dan. "That big sexy is going to keep an eye on me."

Anne playfully hit Kale. "That's my job."

Alex was lying on the blanket, using Komptin as a pillow. "When do you leave, Robbie?"

Robbie dropped a bomb. "We're all moving a week after graduation."

"What?" Dan was shocked, but then he was quiet as he understood the reasoning.

"It's just too hard with dad gone and losing Sara didn't help." Robbie fought back his tears. "So, we're moving back to Minnesota. Mom got a good job; Jennifer is graduating, so it just makes sense."

Anne hugged Kale as if she didn't want to let him go out of fear. Alex was playing with her own hair, thinking of the time Sara helped her weave it in. Alex just stared at the clear sky, almost as if the purple star was shining directly on her. "Her dad

80

won't hurt her anymore." A feeling of guilt came over her as she failed to protect her best friend.

"Did they ever find his body?" Dan asked as he grabbed a beer from the cooler.

"Nope," Mole adjusted himself. "The deputy I'm reporting to stated it was like he completely disappeared." He tensed up a bit.

"Are you okay?" Anne whispered to him.

"It's going to hurt when I get up, but I wouldn't give this up for the life of me." Kale kissed her.

Robbie saw it was getting late. "I need to get going. Take care of Sara, will ya, dad?" He pounded his chest before pointing to the stars.

"You're my ride." Dan collected the cooler. "See you all at graduation."

"Later, stud," Mole said to his friend.

"Drive safe, Robbie," Alex yelled to him.

Alex, Kale, and Anne just sat there on the field. No one really wanted to say a word. Mole was the first to break the silence. "You wanna know something?"

"What's that?" Alex continued to stare at the stars.

"It's really cool that we are all going to be together, even though all three of us will be in different schools." Mole squeezed Anne's hands.

Alex got a sick feeling in her stomach. There was a good chance she wouldn't be with her friends...her family. They continued to sit on the empty football field. Each of them kept quiet as they went through their memories of the past and worries about the future. Alex adjusted her body. The movement caused her phone to move into her side. She pulled it out to see that she had a message in her email. "Damn it." She accidentally said out loud.

"What's wrong, sweetie?" Anne still didn't want to let go of Kale.

"I have a meeting with the principal at eight," Alex told them.

"Why?" Mole inquired.

Alex knew, but she needed to play it off as if she didn't know.

CHAPTER EIGHT

After Alex watched Anne leave with Mole to bring him home, she didn't miss the sense of the Dark that led her to the bleachers. She put down the blanket she was holding on the first set of benches. The air was cold for a late spring. Alex knew there was going to be a hunt tonight. She just wished it wasn't at the school. The Lite Sentry zipped up her leather vest. The hunt was on.

Alex used her skills to find the start of the scent. It was so faint, almost as if it was a Demon scent. If that was the case, she had a harder night ahead of her. She followed the scent under the bleachers of the school on the visitor's side. The support beams became obstacles of metal. She weaved through them rather fluently. There was some black movement about. Then, a blast of Dark hit her senses.

There was no more hunting from the trail. The Dark was close enough now to be too strong to follow. Now, it was just a mission to find it. She knew it was here, no doubt about it. The hunter continued to move through the metallic maze, keeping an eye out for the Dark. Komptin was stalking slowly on the outside of the bleachers.

Then, just as Alex got a sense of that different form of Dark, a flash of red eyes appeared on the other end of the bleachers. Alex motioned for Komptin to follow it. He flashed his eyes just as quickly as he took off. Alex went to start as well but was grabbed by Infiltrator claws from above from in between the bleachers.

It was squeezing her throat with all its might. Alex quickly used her force to jump in the air and fall to the ground. The beast tried to hold on but hit its head on the corner bleacher. The Sentry ran outside the bleachers just in time to see the black beast jump off the back of the metal staircase. As he tackled her, they both rolled while tangled up with each other.

Alex was the first to jump to her feet. She kicked it in the jaw and sent it flying backward onto the ground. There was an advantage to stomping on its head, but her foot was caught. The Infiltrator pushed her foot upwards, causing her to lose her balance, it tackled her, pushing her into a tree. Alex grunted from the pain of her body being sandwiched against the hard surface. The beast wrapped his claws around the tree and kept smashing her against the tree multiple times. Each hit was taking its toll on her.

She slithered her arms inside of the monster's grasp. This gave her the opportunity to slip out of her dire situation. She dropped to her knee, trying to gain her bearings. The bear-like creature attacked her without remorse, knocking and keeping her on her back. Alex immediately head-butted the creature straight in the nose. The creature staggered back, giving Alex the room to stand up.

The bear-like creature lunged at her, but she grabbed its arm, using its own momentum against itself. The Infiltrator slammed into the back of a bleacher beam. It left an imprint from its body hitting the post. The two of them took a moment to regain their strength. The beast went crawling up the back of the bleachers. Alex knew better than to follow it. If she crawled up after him, once it got to the top before her, it would have a significant advantage. She decided to go around.

Alex made it around the corner. The Dark soldier was not on the bleachers. There was no sign of it. Then, from the corner of her eye, she saw it run across the field on all fours to the home bleachers, which were made of stone and much higher. Alex took off following it at full sprint. The Infiltrator hopped onto the cemented benches to run up to the top, near the announcer booth. Alex was at the bottom of the bleachers, standing on the track that circled the football field. She stared at it for a bit. "What are you doing?" She said to herself. Alex watched as it just stood there, staring at her.

Alex very cautiously climbed up the railing to the bottom of the walkway of the viewing area. The beast moved to the other side of the bleachers. Alex stepped onto the first step, as the creature stepped down a step. They mimicked each other until the two met in the middle. "Now what?" The stupidity of the creature's actions perplexed Alex. In an instant, it lunged at her as Alex was in a very vulnerable position. If she lost her balance and began rolling down these stairs, it would cause tremendous pain with every turn, so she just stepped up out of the way. When the creature landed, she kicked it in its side; it was the one that got sent down the bleachers. Its body slammed against the

85

bottom railing. Alex calmly made it down to the bottom bleachers with her eyes glowing and fists lit.

The Infiltrator shook off its cobwebs. Alex could sense its weakened state. The Infiltrator was wobbly as it stared at Alex with hate. It gave a final roar before Komptin jumped from behind it in his gargoyle-hunting form. Its head was engulfed in Komptin's mouth while the body dropped to the ground, before disappearing into the ground.

Alex made it off the bleachers to meet her hunting partner. "Just because you got the final kill, doesn't give you the credit." Alex teased him. The two of them started to get back to the car when a new set of headlights arrived in the parking lot. Alex and Komptin hid behind a nearby dumpster. It was Mr. Dupel. What was he doing here so late?

Alex watched him get out of his car. He mysteriously started into the school on this late night. She put her hunting skills to work as she quietly stayed behind him. There was still a hint of the Dark in the area. Alex caught that sense immediately. Infiltrators and Demons had the same sense, only Demons were fainter. Alex had to get close to him. Maybe he was a Demon. It would explain his actions to prevent her from attending her Catholic college.

She made sure not to follow too closely as she watched him enter the building. She peeked into the door to see the guidance counselor make it down the hallway. Only the emergency lights were on. She gently tugged on the door, but it was locked. "Never easy." She motioned to Komptin that she was going up the fire escape. She could tell he didn't like that, as he couldn't follow her. With much hesitation, he took off to secure the perimeter while she went inside.

Alex made it all the way to the roof, checking every door and window along the way. Of course, not one of them was open. Granted, it would have been easier just to force them open, but one, she didn't feel like damaging school property. And two, she didn't want the alarm going off. Alex made it to the roof, where there were multiple cigarette butts on the ground from faculty sneaking a smoke. That was a good sign. That meant there was a door around here somewhere.

Alex scanned the area to find a door next to the air conditioning unit. "Oh please, oh please, oh please," she said multiple times. She turned the knob to the door to a pleasant surprise. "Yippee." She thought it must have been a safety feature or something not to lock from the outside. Unfortunately, the stairwell was completely black. Even with her ability, it was difficult to see. Luckily, she was a human flashlight.

She felt that weird sense of the Dark again. For sure, it wasn't an Infiltrator or Demon. She ignited her fists to see a mist in the shape of a small man with wings. It flashed its red eyes at Alex before disappearing through the walls into the school. Alex, in turn, flashed her eyes as she opened the door into the empty school.

Alex opened the door that led to a maintenance room of the school. She had a pretty good idea where she was in the building. There was a mixture of that fog thing and a feeling of Darkness from an

Infiltrator. Alex could have sworn she saw that creature before. She continued without having much cover, so she decided to stay in the middle of the hallway. Any Infiltrator could be in the crevice of the doorway that led to each classroom.

"Alex." Her name seemed to be called. She quickly turned her head. She had heard that voice before. During her virgin hunt, the night Robbie's dad was killed. She continued to make it down the hallway. "You have abandoned them." Alex quickly turned around with her fist lit. There was nothing there, but it seemed to be closer. There was no poker face with Alex; it was quite clear she was getting irritated. She continued to head down the hallway. "You will leave them alone for Vandor."

"That's it." Alex was now sauntering with her fist illuminating the hallway. "Get out of my head, you Dark piece of sh–" Alex turned the corner where she ran into Mr. Dupel.

"Alex, what are you doing here?" Mr. Dupel quivered in his voice. "Now we're going to add criminal trespass to your little meeting tomorrow."

Alex took a moment to scan the area. She still couldn't sense any Dark in him. She needed him to use his power to see it. Then, she could dispose of his sorry ass. "What are you doing here?"

He held a planned parenthood brochure. "Taking care of a little problem."

"You truly are a piece of work. You know that, right?" Alex backed up from him.

"I'm not going to hurt you, Alex. Trust me, you'll see what I am capable of tomorrow morning. And if you keep on getting involved with my life, I won't stop at you. Your brother and his little girlfriend aren't that far off from you on my watch list."

"You're an ass." Alex stared at him; she looked deep into his eyes. "The worst part, I don't think you don't have anything in you."

"Be careful what you say tomorrow during your little meeting." Then Mr. Dupel's eyes got big, as if he saw something behind Alex.

Alex turned around to see that fog thing that hung around Vandor. "That's where I know you from," Alex snapped her fingers and pointed at the creature. Her thought was interrupted by Mr. Dupel screaming down the hall in a high screech. "Really? Chickenshit!" She yelled in his direction. She turned back to figure floating down the hall from her position. She was calm when asking, "You going to tell me your name." The dark fog figure just floated in front of her without saying a word, but Alex wasn't really worried. If it was going to attack her, it would have already. "This is going to be a long night if we just stare at each other. What's your name?"

The figure spoke but had no mouth. "My master calls me Salamor."

The tone of his voice was the same as she heard earlier. "So, that's your M.O.; you talk in people's heads, play on their doubts."

"It is easy; primates are so simple-minded." Salamor floated in front of her.

"So, you influenced Mr. Dupel to do all that to me?" Alex used her thumb to point in the direction the guidance counselor ran off.

89

Salamor laughed. "That primate didn't need any pushing; his heart was black enough. Not what I'm looking for."

"Then, what are you looking for?" Alex approached the mist.

The dark spirit never answered. It just flashed its eyes as if studying Alex. "My master will not believe me if I told him, you cannot be converted, but he would be equally as happy upon your death."

Alex turned from the sound of a low growl as another patch of black mist formed into an Infiltrator. "Hmmm," Alex said in a short burst before turning back to Salamor.

"If you live, I will see you again, Lite whore." Salamor started to disappear. "...if you live."

Alex turned to face the Infiltrator. It was slowly stalking up to her, getting ready to pounce. "I have an early meeting tomorrow, so let's get on with this." Alex slammed her fist against the locker. Her fist lit upon impact.

The Infiltrator jumped at Alex; she just stepped to the side. The Infiltrator slid on the hallway floor. It slipped a couple of times before catching grip. It charged Alex again; she punched the beast on top of its head. The force smashed the bottom of its chin against the cemented floor. "Hurts, doesn't it?" The beast grabbed the back of her ankles and dropped Alex on her back. She hit the back of her head on the same floor. "Yep, it does." Alex pulled her leg out and kicked the beast in the face.

The two of them both backed off each other. They both stood up on both their legs. The beast screeched. Alex shot it with a Lite Beam, pushing it back against the wall. She ran towards it while she continued to shoot the beam at it. She shut it off before kneeing it in the stomach. The sound of hollowed lockers echoed through the empty hallways. The Infiltrator elbowed Alex on the side of the head. It followed with a punch in the kidneys.

Alex flinched from the hit. The beast smashed her head against the locker. Alex swung around and hit it with the back of her fist. It stunned the creature long enough for Alex to grab it and head-butt it in the nose. Then it hugged the Lite Sentry and spun around, landing on top of Alex on the floor. She hid her face in the side of the Infiltrator's body to prevent it from biting her. They rolled around on the floor a bit until they both rolled down the stairs, slamming against the landing wall.

The Infiltrator picked Alex up and threw her down the stairs onto the next floor down. Alex got up checking her lip to see how bad it was bleeding. Off the corner of her eye, she was able to see the Infiltrator jump down from the stairs at her. She quickly moved out of the way. Alex grabbed the head of the Infiltrator while still in the air and slammed it to the ground. She kicked it in its side. Upon going for a second kick, the beast grabbed her foot. It stood up while still holding onto her foot.

"Oh shit." Alex knew the hit was coming, and it would hurt. The impact swung her around, and she was met with another punch, knocking her down to the ground. This time, her mouth and lip were pouring out blood. The Infiltrator approached, and Alex smashed its knees with her foot. The cracking sound sent the Infiltrator to the ground. Alex jumped in the air and landed on the Infiltrator's chest with her knee. She continued to punch the Infiltrator until she sensed it was weakened enough to dispose. She formed a pointed Lite weapon on her fist and stabbed it in the chest. The Infiltrator howled in pain as it disappeared into the floor.

Alex just dropped to the ground and then rolled over on her back. "I thought they were supposed to get easier." She had a mixture of laughter and crying from the pain she was in. Alex didn't know how long she lay there before getting up to go back to the roof to get to the fire escape and get out of the school. As soon as she hit the ground, she was greeted by a purple-skinned gargoyle. "Where were you?" Alex teased him as she scratched his ears. "Come on, I need to get cleaned up before I lose my scholarship."

***

Alex wasn't late. She was standing outside the principal's office with an ice pack pressed against her lip. It was just about eight hours ago she was in this school, destroying an Infiltrator. Now, she is back in it, about to lose her scholarship. She didn't really want her last moment in this school to be a bad one.

The doorknob turning seemed to take forever before the principal called Alex in. "Come on, Ms. Johnson." Alex followed her into an office, where Mr. Dupel was standing in the corner of the office. "No parents?"

"I'm eighteen, and there is nothing that you are going to say that I can't repeat to them. So lay it on me. I'm ready." Alex just stood her ground.

"You don't seem very scared. Have a seat, Ms. Johnson." Principal Sapp observed.

Alex glared directly at Mr. Dupel. "Just because I'm scared, doesn't cause me to scream out of the building like a little girl." Alex felt good with that as she slowly sat down, ready to receive her news.

"Well, we looked over transcripts, and obviously, you know that the college where you applied has a GPA standard that you fall short of, yet you still got sponsored. They were willing to overlook that, but the report from Mr. Dupel about your fighting and, shall we say, your reputation of friendliness, has some concerns for that particular school." Principal Sapp looked over her record. "It has been documented that you averaged three fights per school year, and those are the ones just on school grounds."

"Never started any of them." Alex thought it was the defense she had.

"Regardless, your choice in handling confrontation is yet to be desired per Mr. Dupel," Principal Sapp told her. "We cannot put our name as a school as an endorsement of you under these conditions."

"So, you're saying the reputation of your school might be affected; that's rich." Alex prevented herself from crying by turning her head towards the ceiling.

93

The door opened to the principal's office, and Brooke was escorted with Father Hanley behind her. There were two other people with her, who Alex assumed were Brooke's parents. Alex made sure to see Mr. Dupel, who was white as a ghost. "This should be good," Alex all of a sudden had all her stress alleviated. She sat back in her chair to enjoy the show.

"Ms. Thompson, what's going on? This is a private meeting." Principal Sapp was now standing up. By the tone in her voice, it was evident she didn't enjoy the interruption.

Mr. Dupel started heading out of the office, but Father Hanley stepped in front of him. "Don't you even think of leaving this room. Do you hear me?" He had his hand on Mr. Dupel's chest. Mr. Dupel was in a fight-or-flight mode, so he sat down on a chair in the room.

"What is going on?" Principal Sapp was getting irritated that she was losing control of the situation.

Brooke had a tissue in her hand. She took in a deep breath before speaking. "I'm pregnant, and Mr. Dupel is the father."

Principal Sapp's eyes got wide as she slowly turned her head to the trusted guidance counselor. "What?" Mr. Dupel sank lower in his chair.

Brooke's parents hovered over their daughter. Brooke swallowed hard. "I told Alex and made her promise not to tell anyone. Mr. Dupel found out she knew and threatened her to ruin her school scholarship."

"Along with Anne McClure and Kale Moler's." Alex just thought she would add a little fuel to the fire. It wasn't much, but Alex couldn't help herself.

"That is why you were holding off on signing Anne's 1046?" Principal Sapp was now getting visibly angry. "Ms. Johnson, I can assure you. You will be attending your college next year. Anne and Mr. Moler will be fine as well."

Alex smiled as a victory had just fallen on her lap. "Thank you."

Father Hanley tapped Alex on the shoulder. "We should go," he whispered in her ear.

Alex swiftly nodded in agreement as she gathered her belongings to leave the school with Father Hanley. They both left the building with Komptin at Alex's side. "Thanks for that. How long did you know?"

"For a while, but I was confined by my vows." Father Hanley felt as if a burden of stress was lifted off his shoulders.

"I get it," Alex turned around to the school. "Thanks." A mixture of fear and accomplishment ran through her as she turned to the school. This was the last time she was going to be in that building as a student.

The priest nodded. "But Alex," Father Hanley brought her back to reality. "The damage is done. I know Carl. He is strict and does care for people who beat the system. I can confidently tell you; he already doesn't like you."

Alex grabbed an Apollo from her book bag. "Well, I'm sure I will never run into him."

CHAPTER NINE

Alex was sitting in the congregation room drinking an Apollo. This time, she was not alone. Mole and Anne were there as well. Mole wanted to sit in the pews, but the hard, wooden benches were a little much on his back, so he just stayed in the wheelchair. Of course, Anne was on his lap. "Bummer, you didn't make valedictorian, Anne."

"I'm not." Anne still held her academic achievement pin in her hand. "Tim deserved it. He's really smart and studied all the time. Plus, that's all he did. While my focus was the school itself, I wanted to make it better for the next person."

"That's my girl, always thinking of making the world better." Mole played with her hair. He got a message on his phone that his mom was out in the parking lot. "I gotta go. Graduation party."

"I'll be there in a bit," Anne told him. "I have to make an appearance at a couple of others."

Alex watched as Mole rolled away. "I feel guilty that I don't tell him the truth about what I do."

"Sometimes ignorance is truly bliss." Anne put a different perspective to Alex's statement. "Is everything set for your graduation party?"

"Yes, after services on Sunday, so we don't have to rush to clean up." Alex let her know.

"Why here?" Anne sat down next to Alex.

Alex closed her eyes. "Can't you feel the warmth? It's so peaceful." Alex then opened her eyes. "Plus, I really don't want any Dark to ruin this." She tapped Anne on the leg. "I'm really happy the three of us are going to be together."

"Me too, sweetie." Anne smiled. "It was a rough year."

"It was. I'm sure the future ahead is going to be a lot more rough." Alex stared at the stained-glass window.

Anne got a message from Kale on her phone. "That's why the world has Alexandria Johnson as a Lite Sentry." She got up from the pew. "I have to go. Kale left his diploma in my car." She went down the aisle and stopped to turn around to her friend. "Alex, I just want you to know that having Kale and you in my life, really makes me feel like I'm complete. I look at you like family."

Alex blushed. "You and Mole are such a Hallmark couple."

"You'll have yours someday." Anne teased her. "I have to go, sweetie."

"Nope, never. No Hallmark Christmas special for this girl." Alex laughed. "Now get out of here. I'll see you at your party."

The two of them said their goodbyes. Alex had a couple of moments to herself before heading out to all the graduation parties. It was peaceful. The church was quiet, and Alex closed her eyes to enjoy the quiet warmth of the sanctuary. It truly was a moment of Zen.

"Am I disturbing you, Alexandria?" Celestial quietly asked her Lite Sentry.

Alex always welcomed a visit from Celestial. "Never." Alex got up to give her a quick bow.

"It was nice to see your commencement," Celestial put her hand on her Lite Sentry's cheek.

"I don't know about that, but I graduated today." Alex pointed out.

Celestial prevented herself from smirking too much. "Yes. Congratulations. I understand it is customary to give a gift on such an occasion."

"You don't have to," Alex was secretly wondering what she could possibly give her.

"But I will," Celestial's face got serious. "A little advice. The Demon Myst Vandor, called Salamor; he is far more dangerous than you realize. His ability of mind manipulations is not something to take with no care."

"Good thing I'm pretty hard-headed." Alex knocked on her skull. "Though, I know an Infiltration did take place recently. I will find it and destroy it."

"I know you will," Celestial put her hand on her Lite Sentry's head. "But I actually do have something to give to you."

"Okay," Alex, for some reason, was a little leery. The Conduit of Lite reached behind her and gave her a box with a door on it. Alex cautiously took possession of it. She studied it immensely.

"Remember, every door presented for you to open; it is ultimately up to you to decide if you are going to accept what is on the other side." Celestial waited to see what Alex was going to do next.

Alex took the box with one hand. She used two fingers to slowly open the box. Inside, a Christmas ornament was hanging from the top. The light blue ornament had a Hallmark crown sprinkled with glitter. Alex took the ornament out of the box and studied it. "Thank you." She didn't know what else to say.

Celestial beamed with delight as if she had a secret. "That is all you need to know."

Alex put the ornament back in the box. She watched as Celestial opened the conduit to the Lite. The angel disappeared into the Lite. Ariel and Devine started to follow her but stopped to face Alex. They spoke at the same time, "We put our names on with hers." They both went into the conduit. Alex just gave them both a lip-tight smile as they left.

Upon the Conduit closing, Alex just sat there for a bit, basking in the thoughts about her life ahead of her. She held the box that contained her ornament under her arm. Komptin joined her, sitting down faithfully by her side. "Well, we have the summer ahead of us. What do you want to do?" Komptin flashed his eyes. "Yah, me too." She laughed as the two of them sauntered out of the congregation room together. They took with them the memories of yesterday that prepared them for the challenges of tomorrow.

The End